That sad little house was her sister's home

"Don't cry for Regan," Drew said harshly. "She wouldn't thank you for pitying her. She has more happiness in that wee house than we have in our mansion, and probably more than you have in yours."

Rowan leaned her head against the gate and tried to stop her tears, as he continued, "Regan has different values from most people's. She's not materialistic. She has no envy in her makeup, no jealousy. She's the happiest person I know."

And you love her, Rowan thought, feeling bruised and empty.

"Of course," he went on in that pitiless voice, "you wouldn't understand. You two are only alike on the outside—on the inside you're quite different. Regan's a decent kid, Rowan. She isn't your kind at all."

Springs of Love

Mary Moore

Harlequin Books

TORONTO • NEW YORK • LONDON
AMSTERDAM • PARIS • SYDNEY • HAMBURG
STOCKHOLM • ATHENS • TOKYO • MILAN

Original hardcover edition published in 1983
by Mills & Boon Limited

ISBN 0-373-02606-4

Harlequin Romance first edition March 1984

CHAPTER ONE

ROWAN Chapman slowly came awake. She could hear her parents' voices by the pool. Of course, it was Saturday and Daddy would be home. She stretched luxuriously. What a fantastic party! Last night had been her coming-of-age, her twentieth birthday. And Greg had proposed. She giggled, thinking how formal he had been—quite romantic.

He had insisted on asking her parents' permission, and incredibly they had asked them to *wait*. It was quite ridiculous, really, twenty was just the right age for a girl, and Greg was much older. Many of her friends were married, after all.

She pushed back the quilt and stood up. A slender girl of medium height with soft brown shoulder-length hair, vivid blue eyes and vivacious, heart-shaped face. She ran to the sundeck and leaned over. 'Hi, you early birds. I thought you'd be sleeping off the party.'

'Morning, Princess.' Her father waved back. 'Ready for breakfast?'

'Do you want a swim first?' her mother asked. 'There's nothing to spoil, just fruit and cereal. It won't take a moment to make fresh toast.'

'Think I will,' Rowan called and quickly pulled on her brief bikini which showed her trim, tanned figure to perfection. As she ran a comb through her naturally curly hair, she addressed the mirror. 'Talk about your average Kiwi, I must be it. Average height, average weight, average brain, average looks—what does Greg see in me?' She looked around her beautiful bedroom which her parents had had specially redecorated for her birthday, then poked her tongue out at her reflection.

'Stupid.' Her mouth curved into an attractive smile. 'He's marrying me because I have the most super parents in the whole wide world. I knew there had to be a reason.' She ran lightly down the outside stairs and, dropping her towelling wrap by the pool, swam a vigorous ten lengths before pulling herself gasping up on the edge.

'Whew! That was fantastic—I feel a new man!'

'If the Human Rights should hear you, my darling daughter, you'd be for it. Not a new man, nor yet a new woman, but you may declare yourself to be a new person.'

'I'll settle for that.' Rowan rolled over and on to her feet in one lithe movement. She rubbed her hair dry, then slipped on her robe before joining them at the table. Her bright blue eyes surveyed them lovingly, and she noticed how young they looked.

'I was just thinking, up in the room, I've got the best parents in the world, and that must be why Greg wants to marry me.'

'Thanks for the compliment, but you underestimate yourself,' her father said with a laugh.

'Maybe, but I don't underestimate my luck that you two chose me out of all the unwanted babies. I sort of don't think about it much, then sometimes it hits me such a wallop. Like last night—all the razzmatazz you turned on for me must have cost you a small fortune. And the tables piled with presents. You know, I've got enough to set up a home of my own, probably two.'

'Our pleasure, Princess. And all our friends wanted to celebrate with us. You've given us nothing but joy ever since we brought you home from the hospital. Other people's babies cried at night, got bellyache, and all the rest, but our baby was just perfect,' her father declared.

Rowan grinned. 'I *never* cried?'

'Can't remember it.'

'You did,' her mother admitted, 'but rarely. You had a very sweet and loving nature, and you still have.'

'I think I might be about to lose it unless you two have some reasonable explanation as to why you refused to give your consent to Greg and me getting engaged. Don't you think I'm old enough? You can't have anything against Greg. You've known him all your lives—he's the son of your best friends—and we've been going around together for simply ages. You'd have said something before now if you had objected to him?'

'That's true enough,' her father replied. 'We'll talk about it when you've had your breakfast.' He returned to reading his paper.

Rowan didn't push. It would be no use—she knew her father well enough by now.

Her mother made fresh tea and toast and poured a cup for herself as well as for Rowan. 'Were you very upset, dear? We didn't mean to hurt you.'

'No. I'm not hurt, just puzzled.' She bit into her toast. 'To be quite honest, I'm worried about how I'm not more worried, if you know what I mean. Greg and I have dated off and on for years, we're happy together, and last night seemed a good time. I've finished my kindergarten training and there're no jobs around. We've always expected to marry, so why not now? Yet, in a strange way, I'm pleased you made us wait. Why? Is it because I don't really love him? I should be wailing and gnashing my teeth, and I'm perfectly serene. You're both doctors: explain me to me.'

Her father glanced significantly at her mother, then asked, 'Have you finished eating?'

'Not quite. I'm hungry, which is crazy after all that rubbish I ate last night. The food was scrumptious.'

She winked at her mother as she saw her father return to his paper. He was so predictable that it made her feel very secure. He would talk to her when she finished her breakfast and not before then.

Her mother smiled reprovingly, and shook her head, so Rowan concentrated on her meal. She wasn't in that much of a hurry. She looked at the beautiful house that was her home, the sweep of lawns and the well-tended garden, and then further beyond to the beautiful Waitemata Harbour. She loved Auckland, she loved her home, and she loved her parents—and she was fairly sure she loved Greg. Did all adopted kids feel this well of gratitude for their parents? She knew some kids went berserk trying to find their natural parents, but she had never wanted to.

She jumped up and cleared the patio table and carried the dishes through to the kitchen, rinsing them and placing them in the dishmaster. She returned and took the cloth off, shook the crumbs over her father to notify him she had finished breakfast, then skipped smartly out of his way.

'Ready to parley, Papa?' she asked with a grin.

'You ungrateful brat,' he grumbled, brushing the crumbs off his lean, tanned stomach. 'I've a good mind to wait until after lunch.'

'But you won't, will you?' she coaxed. 'I'm going for a picnic with Greg and the crowd, and I'd die of curiosity before I got back.'

'Considering the cost of funerals, I may relent.' He looked again in that significant way at his wife. 'Do you want to start, or shall I?'

'You, dear, you've got a better way with words than me.'

Rowan propped her head on her elbows and narrowed her eyes. This was going to be something quite serious, she sensed it. Surely they weren't going to tell her about her natural parents. They would probably only do that if it had some connection with Greg. Did they know who her parents were? Golly, she hoped she wasn't related to Greg, or something ghastly like that. She waited quietly, knowing from experience that her father would take his time, anyhow.

He cleared his throat. 'Well, Rowan, you're twenty

years of age. In present times that means you are considered an adult with, presumably, responsibility for your own actions from here on. Your mother and I agreed the day we brought you home that on the day you reached your majority we would give you some information about your background . . .'

'I don't want to know. You are my mother and father, and that's it.'

'We have decided that this is also important because it concerns a promise we made your mother twenty years ago. We did not make this promise lightly. You will know us both well enough: having given our word, we wish to discharge our obligation. Now, will you permit it?'

Rowan bit her lip. How like her father to ask her to be willing to receive it instead of just telling her. 'Will it alter my life, knowing this news?'

'Yes,' her father answered without hesitation. 'It altered ours. It depends on how you accept it. You may ignore it entirely, or you may want to follow it up. We will not criticise your decision either way.'

'My life is extremely pleasant just as it is,' Rowan muttered. 'Okay, get on with it. I can't leave you both stuck with your obligation.

'When we made application to adopt we had to wait a considerable time. We have already described our preparations and our excitement when we were told our baby had actually arrived. It was a most wonderful day. What we did not tell you was that, when we arrived at the Maternity Hospital, we were interviewed by the Matron. Owing to extremely unusual circumstances, and your mother's state of mind, she had decided to pass on to us a request which would ease a little of the stress your mother was undergoing. Apparently, your mother unexpectedly gave birth to twins—it had not been discovered until the actual birth.'

'*Twins*! I'm a twin?' Rowan gasped.

'Yes. The couple who arrived to accept the first baby were asked could they possibly take two, to keep you together. They refused, and there was no question of them returning to Auckland again because they had had a very expensive journey to get there. When we heard, we naturally wanted both babies. We offered to travel down and pay all expenses, but this was also refused. For your mother's peace of mind, the Matron asked us to promise that we would one day tell you and that maybe you would meet each other. We gave that promise, but we were unable to have the name or address of the other couple. All we know is that they came from one of the country districts in Nelson.'

'But I'll never find my other half with only that little bit to go on,' Rowan wailed. 'They could have moved. The baby may have died. Was it a girl or a boy?'

'A girl. You have a sister. You have only one way of knowing who she is—she was an identical twin. She will be a mirror likeness of you, but you won't have her name or anything else to help you.'

'And didn't you make any enquiries at the time? You could have found her so easily then and kept track of her for me.'

'No, we were not allowed to do that. That was one condition she insisted on. We were supposed to wait until you were twenty-one, but that was when legal coming-of-age was twenty-one. Also, with your talking about becoming engaged . . .'

Rowan interrupted her father impatiently, 'Don't tell me I wasn't to be told if I got married! How could my getting engaged upset things?'

'That was an entirely separate issue. We still have to discuss it. Your turn, Elizabeth.'

Her mother's smile was sweet. 'Before that, tell me, dear, are you pleased with the news? Or does it upset you?'

'Upset me?' Rowan bounced off her chair. 'I'm wild

with excitement. It's the most wonderful present you've ever given me. I can't wait to meet her and talk to her.'

She rushed over to kiss her mother, then her father. Then hugging herself with excitement, she announced, 'I've got to *do something*.' She threw off her robe and plunged into the pool and stroked madly to the other end, crawled out and raced to the trampoline where she bounced and pivoted until she exhausted herself.

She walked slowly back to her parents, overwhelmed by all sorts of emotions. She had always wanted a sister. Imagine if they had grown up together, sharing everything. What if her sister didn't like her? But if they were identical, wouldn't she be just as excited? Oh, bother the picnic, she wanted to start looking now, today.

She sat down on the tiled surround, hugging her knees, her small lively face bright with enthusiasm. 'Does she know I exist? Did the other parents make the same promise? Are they expecting me to come looking? Maybe she is looking for me right now. Oh, I could burst with happiness!'

'Steady down, Princess! One question at a time. Yes, they know you exist. No, they refused to promise anything. And I doubt that they would even tell her. She would have a more difficult time tracing you in a huge city like Auckland.'

'It'll be all the better if it's a surprise,' Rowan said with a grin.

Her father smiled. 'Don't get too wildly excited. It may take you years to trace her. And you'll have to face the fact that you may never find her. You must be realistic. Fifty thousand people emigrated from New Zealand last year, so don't build your hopes too high.'

'How high is too high?' demanded Rowan. 'My hopes are already higher than . . . than the moon. I'll find her, I know I'll find her. I will never give up if it takes me all my life.'

'And Greg? Do you think he will wait patiently for years while you run all over the place?'

'Do you think I'll have to choose?' Rowan was appalled.

'You may well have to, Princess. I don't think he will be at all delighted with the news. He's going to lose you for quite a while. You can't expect immediate results.'

'Then I choose my sister. If Greg waits, that's fine. If he gets mad about it, I'm still going.'

'You sound very positive, Rowan,' her mother said with a lift of her delicately arched eyebrows.

'I am very positive. I have no choice.'

'Tell me, dear, which excites you more, the thought of finding your sister, or the thought of getting married?'

'Mother! How can you ask such a thing? Anyone can get married, but to search for and find someone identical to you in every way . . . why, it's fascinating. You don't know just how excited I am!'

Her father cleared his throat again. 'Now is the time to explain why we asked you and Greg to wait. Your mother and I have watched you two together for a long time. We like Greg, we approve of him, but we have been a trifle worried that you two could drift into marriage because it was expected of you. You've been involved in several minor roles in weddings lately and it is well known that one wedding often leads to another.'

'But I do love Greg!' Rowan protested. 'Well, we've had our troubles, but basically we're, what's the word, compatible.'

'For a young couple verging on marriage, compatible seems to be a fairly tepid description of your relationship.'

'I tempered it down for your ageing ears,' Rowan laughed. 'There are some more contemporary words more fitting, but they are slightly crude. I don't exactly cringe at the thought of him bedding me; the fact that we've shown a commendable restraint is more because of the discussions I've shared with you two on premarital sex, than any lack of desire on my part. He's fun to be with, he stimulates me in all sorts of ways, we hardly ever have any hassles. I call that love and I think it is a good basis for marriage.'

'I think so, too,' her father agreed. 'Yet I find something missing. It's hard to put into words, yet your mother and I had it, and we know it's not there with you and Greg. It's a spark, a divine spark, that stirs the spirit and soul, it's an inner knowledge of each other, that rapture and pure delight which binds with unbreakable cords the hearts of those who truly love each other. I would hate you to miss it, Princess.'

'How do you know we haven't got it? We're pretty close . . . we harmonise.'

'Yes, you do. And I'm not suggesting that what you've got isn't very good indeed, nor that it won't develop into something far deeper. I am just saying that marriage is a lifetime commitment, the for richer, for poorer part, the in sickness and in health part, the for better, for worse part: all tremendously large promises, and we honestly don't think you are quite ready for them yet. If what you feel for each other is genuine and lasting, then it will not diminish by your being apart for a few months. In fact it will grow, and you will be much more sure of each other when you exchange your vows.'

'Let me get this straight,' Rowan's blue eyes were intent. 'You're really asking me to make no promises at all to Greg for a few months . . . how many months, exactly, did you have in mind?'

'Make it six months. A time of testing, but nothing worth having is lightly gained.'

'And you agree with him, Mummy?'

'I'm afraid I do, Rowan. You almost admitted it yourself when you said you found the thought of finding your sister more exciting than marriage.'

'I thought I could have both,' Rowan said a trifle sadly.

'No reason why you can't. But even your reaction to the news was instinctively personal. You didn't yell that you must share it with Greg, or that he'd be wild about the whole thing. You obviously didn't really care what his reaction was, it was a private joy . . . yours. Any two people as close to sharing lives as you two presumably are would have automatically tried to fit their partner into the scheme of things.'

Rowan stood up and walked to the pool, staring down into the blue depths with unseeing eyes. She knew they were right, and it hurt. They had never given bad advice, and they never manipulated her. They always spoke honestly, then left her to her own decision. She knew she could turn around and face them and say that she and Greg were going to go right ahead, and they would accept that without argument. They had spoken their thoughts and she was absolutely free to decide.

She wanted so much to have a marriage like theirs. They blended together, using each other's strengths, making loving allowance for each other's weaknesses. She sighed heavily. If they said she and Greg did not have that completeness in each other, but that it could grow, then she would rather wait and find it. She trusted their judgment.

She turned towards them. 'What if I go down South and I lose him?'

Her mother met her gaze steadily. 'Would you rather not know?'

Rowan picked up her towel. 'No. If his love for me won't survive six months, then it wouldn't be that abiding love you talk about. I'll talk it over with him . . . it's as much his decision as mine. We can still write, I suppose?'

'Make your own rules,' her father said quietly. 'He can go down to see you, you can fly home for a weekend, you can phone each other daily if you want to. We only suggest that you do not make a final commitment to marriage for six months.'

'I'll get ready for the picnic.' She started up the stairs, then leaning over the rail, said, 'If I lose him it will kill me. I can't imagine life without Greg in it—he's always *been* there.'

Her father smiled. 'If you feel like that, then you're almost there. If Greg feels like that, then you *are* there.'

'I guess so,' Rowan said uncertainly. 'I surely hope you're right.'

'So do we.'

By the time she had changed into shorts and suntop and packed some goodies, her mood had lifted and she ran out to meet Greg, her small lively face lit with excitement.

'I've just got so much to tell you, Greg, darling. You'll never believe what news I have.'

He pulled her close and kissed her expertly, then as they drove off, said with a smile, 'Your parents have relented. We're to be married immediately.'

Rowan felt a huge wave of guilt sweep her as she realised her thoughts had all been on her new quest, and not on postponing the wedding. She looked at Greg's handsome face, wondering how she could best put it to him.

She snuggled up to him. 'Not exactly, but they really only want us to wait six months. That's not a long time, darling!'

He drove skilfully through the city towards the isolated beach where the gang were meeting. 'Six months! You're right, it's not long. We can accommodate them. It would probably take that long to make all the arrangements.'

'No. They didn't mean the wedding in six months. They want us not to make any commitment to each other for six months. They only want us to be really sure.'

'Aren't you sure, Rowan?' He flicked a puzzled glance at her.

'Of course I'm sure. It's just a matter of proving to them that we are ready for marriage. I'd like to please them, if the thought of waiting doesn't appal you too much.'

'You're one of a kind, Rowan. You come out lit up like a Christmas tree, then tell me I'm to wait another six months or longer before I have the right to call you my own. Still, it will suit me, actually. My work-load at the firm is getting pretty heavy, and it would be wise to get the seasonal rush over before we marry. I agree, if you agree.'

'*I do love you, Greg,*' Rowan said thankfully. But she thought ruefully that she would have been more flattered if he had protested a little more forcefully. And she wasn't one of a kind . . . not any more, but it was one of his favourite expressions concerning her. There were only a few more miles to the beach, and she had to tell him her news before they joined the others.

She took a deep breath and plunged in, 'I've got the most incredible news, Greg. I've been dying to tell you. I know you'll be wildly excited about it, too. My parents told me this morning that when they adopted me, there was another baby . . . that I'm really a twin. I have a sister somewhere, an exact replica of me.'

Greg had an unpleasant scowl on his good-looking face. 'Why didn't they adopt you both?'

'They couldn't, someone else had already taken my sister. Mum and Dad tried, but it was impossible. They both think I should use these few months to go to the South Island and see if I can find her.'

'Rubbish! That's the most stupid thing I've ever heard of. You've grown up in a completely different environment, and you'll have nothing in common. You're not really thinking of going?'

'Yes, I am. Oh, Greg, please try and understand,' Rowan pleaded with a sinking heart. If Greg got into one of his moods, the whole day would be horrible.

'I don't understand, and I'm not going to try. You've got everything going for you here. What will you gain meeting some unknown girl and complicating her life and yours? It's a stupid romantic notion. Forget it.'

'I can't do that, Greg. I can't.'

'I am prepared to put off the wedding, but not if you're going haring off down South, chasing a will-o'-the-wisp. They shouldn't have told you, and I thought they would have had more wisdom. Your life is here; you have them, you have me, you have loads of friends—you don't need anyone else! That's my final word. I don't want to discuss it any further.'

Tears burned in Rowan's eyes. She knew Greg—he was awfully stubborn. What was she going to do? She had thought he would be angry about putting off the wedding, but he had taken it so casually, as if it was of no real consequence. But the thing that was really important to her, the search for her sister, he would not countenance. Perhaps if she did everything to please him today, and did not mention anything about her sister, they might be able to talk it over quietly when they got home. She hadn't chosen the time well, that was it. She had been silly, springing it on him suddenly. But they had just this hour together before they joined the crowd. She thought they could have talked about it sensibly, shared ideas of how she should go about it. Obviously, she had been very naïve.

'Move over a bit, Rowan, the road is a bit tricky here,' Greg demanded coldly.

Rowan shifted away from him, feeling completely miserable. The sun streamed down on them, the day was perfect, and yet her heart ached. She hardly ever crossed Greg, but when she did, he made her pay for it. He would totally ignore her today and flirt with Sarah, and Sarah would play up to him the way she always did. Sarah was so beautiful, and she always treated Rowan a little contemptuously, showing that Greg was wasted on such an ordinary girl.

As Greg swung the sports car into the sandy beach, he spoke again in the same cold voice. 'I mean it, Rowan. I am not going to share you with anyone else. You're either all mine, or you're not. You'll have to decide today, so think about it. If you find her, which is barely possible after all these years, and you want to form some sort of relationship with her, you'll be rushing off down there every chance you get, or bringing her up here, cluttering up our lives with someone I don't need. If you don't find her, all our holidays in the future are going to be aimed at hunting another clue in some outlandish place. You either stop it now, before it becomes an obsession and ruins our lives, or we separate, not for six months but for always.'

Rowan could see Sarah sauntering towards them. 'You can't mean that, Greg. Let's both think it over today, and talk about it tonight.'

'No, I've thought it over. If you have no consideration for me, then I think we shouldn't marry. You're being utterly selfish. It's my life too, and I can decide who I want in it, and I don't want your Orphan-Annie sister!'

Rowan sat stunned, watching through a blur of tears as Greg ran towards Sarah, catching her in his arms and bending to kiss her with familiarity that spoke of practice. She saw him strip down to his swimming trunks and kick off his sandals, then he caught Sarah's hand and ran laughing towards the sea.

It couldn't be over so swiftly. He was only punishing her for arguing with him. He sometimes did that, although not often, because she was fairly careful not to provoke him, and she was always acutely aware of how lucky she was to have such a wonderful guy as her steady date.

'Greg in one of his moods, Rowan?' Debbie opened the

car door. 'What's bugging him this time? You two looked like a pair of lovebirds last night.'

Rowan brushed the tears from her eyes. 'Oh Debbie, I feel so miserable. Yesterday was so great, and the party last night was fabulous. I was so happy . . .'

'Come on in for a swim. We've been waiting for you lot. The surf is looking good, so bring your board. I knew there was something up when I saw Greg and Sarah having a pash-up. Care to share the load with me?'

Rowan smiled a little wanly at Debbie, her very best friend. 'No. But thanks. This is something I've got to sort out by myself. Greg's angry with me, and he has every right to be. I've got to think how to put it right.'

'There's only ever one way to put things right with Greg, and that's to go his way. How you can put up with that spoiled brat is beyond me—he twists you round his little finger. You're far too good for him.'

Rowan shook her head in protest. 'How can you say that? He's fabulous. Everybody likes Greg, and you do yourself.'

'Yes, I do, but I'd hate to marry him. More than that, I'd hate to see anyone I liked married to him. He is a natural leader, he's good-looking, he's a top athlete, he's intelligent and charming . . . and he is selfish to the marrowbone. He has no consideration for anyone's point of view except his own. Surely you must have noticed, love can't have made you *that* blind.'

Rowan stared out at the sparkling blue waves where Greg and Sarah were putting on quite a show for the group, and for her. Her mind was in a turmoil.

Suddenly Debbie opened the car door. 'Shove over. I can see by your face that this isn't some ordinary spat, because you look like death. Now tell me what's happened.'

'It's all over. Greg and I are finished, I just know it.' She fought hard to control her tears, then decided to tell

Debbie everything. It was too big to think through by herself.

When she finished Debbie sat quietly for a moment. 'I think you're right, Rowan. If you persist in looking for your sister, you can forget all about Greg. No wonder he's on his high horse. He has to have your undivided attention; he won't stand any competition. You've never looked at another boy, have you?'

'No. I've always been Greg's girl. But this isn't another boy—this is a girl, family even . . .'

'Didn't your parents warn you that Greg might react badly? They are pretty bright as parents go, and they must have seen through him by now.'

Rowan bit her lip, trying to think back to breakfast at the pool, and retracing the conversation. 'Now you mention it, I think that's what they were saying. I didn't take it that way, but they did say I might have to make a choice.'

'There you go,' Debbie said with a sigh of relief. 'I knew I couldn't be wrong about them. He's just not right for you, Rowan.'

'Why are you saying this now?' Rowan glared at her indignantly. 'You've always been perfectly satisfied with the set-up until now.'

'Perfectly satisfied is not correct. I have accepted it, so has the gang, but we've always known he wasn't up to your standard. We've hoped that as you grew up you might question the way he treats you. You're a giver, he's a taker; if you married him you'd always be a small shadow somewhere behind him. He's not even faithful to you, Rowan.'

Colour burned Rowan's cheeks. 'That's my fault and you know it.'

'Oh, come on, don't make excuses for him. You mean just because you won't sleep with him, that gives him licence to have a little flutter on the side when his biological urges get frustrated. Rubbish. You have your principles, I will admit they are a bit unusual in this day and age, but you're not obnoxious about your ideas, and you don't criticise others who behave differently. I know you take a bit of flak from us all, but on the whole we admire you and respect your decision.'

'But men are *different* . . .'

'Some men. Greg certainly is. He's quite proud of the fact that you still have your virginity, but he works the old double standard to his own advantage. He knows you'll forgive his occasional meanderings, and what's worse, blame yourself, and you don't know half of what he gets up to. Do you want to marry a guy like that? Do you think he'll cleave only unto you after you're married?'

'Of course he will.'

'Rubbish. He's a born philanderer. You'll probably hate my guts if you and Greg make up, but I've been waiting a long time to say these things to you. There would have been no point in discussing it before now, you thought him perfect, and were so loyal that you wouldn't even talk about it, but we've often seethed about the treatment he's dished out to you. If you're going to make a big decision, you'd better know how others see him.'

'You're saying I'm immature, I've got no judgment,' Rowan said in a bewildered tone.

'Only as far as Greg goes. You've never looked beneath the surface of his character. He's flawed. You watch him today, with objective eyes, and you'll be surprised at what you see.'

'I'd rather not.'

'You have no choice, unless you're going to forget about this twin of yours. Of course you can do that; you've never needed her before, and she'll never know you even exist, but I think you'd always regret not searching for her.'

'I won't regret it,' Rowan returned forthrightly. 'Because it's the only thing I am certain about at this moment. Let's go for a swim.'

'Now you're talking,' Debbie beamed at her. 'And don't be too certain that after a time Greg won't come crawling back. You're a pretty special person, Rowan, and I think he'll miss you like hell if you go out of his life. We'll miss you, too, if you go. You don't have any conceit, and if the gang had a vote, you'd rate on the popularity scale higher than most, and with me you'd be top.'

'Thanks for the ego trip.' Rowan attempted a shaky grin and ran down to the sea.

The whole day had a strange and unreal quality about it. Rowan swam and surfed with the others, laughed and played games with them, and all the time she watched Greg, trying to analyse her feelings towards him. She had always loved him, and not looked for any faults—not believed he had any, if it came to that. But today it was like looking at one of those paintings in the museum, with lines drawn so that as you stared they alternated between becoming mountains or deep pits—an optical illusion. And as she watched Greg, she saw all the good things about him, all the fun they had shared; then the picture would change and she would become aware of the times he had hurt her, and the mean things he had done to the other members in their loose-knit group.

It seemed that Debbie had opened her eyes so that she saw with new insight into his behaviour, and she was shocked at herself for being so pathetic. She was shocked also that she felt such little emotion. It was not hurting her, because each time she felt depressed, up would bubble the joy at the thought of finding her other half. She knew that she should be equally careful in assessing her chances of success and the eventual outcome of that adventure, but it was impossible. It was the most marvellous thing that had ever happened to her. If she had broken up with Greg at any other time she would have been utterly crushed, now it seemed a very secondary aspect.

Rowan was horrified now at the casual way she had viewed her decision to marry, being more interested in setting up house, planning her wedding dress, thinking of their life together in terms of entertainments and fun. It appeared so superficial. She hated the way less attractive traits in Greg had flicked so easily across her mind: his impatience, his barbed sense of humour. She had always thought herself over-sensitive when she had cringed at some of his remarks, but now she saw clearly that it was his insensitivity which was the problem. He had a scintillating wit, but it was mostly used to denigrate another person's self-esteem, and he specialised in jokes about the Irish, or Jews, or Maoris. He was very clever, and he could make people laugh in spite of themselves, but afterwards you felt slightly ashamed that you had.

Greg had called her sister Little Orphan Annie. Did he think of *her* like that? As the day wore on he was obviously annoyed at a lack of reaction from her to his outrageous behaviour with Sarah, and she found herself becoming the butt of his sarcasm. It was lightly done and terribly amusing, but she had no doubt he meant to wound. Rowan laughed with the others and was amazed to find that his cruelty did not hurt, but made her feel immensely sorry for him.

As they packed up the gear he suddenly switched and, ignoring Sarah, became the tender loving man she had thought him to be. Rowan walked towards the car with him, her mind made up.

'Well, Princess, will we see the parents and tell them we're not prepared to wait six months? Let's get married straight away. I know you better than you know yourself, and you weren't serious about going on a wild-goose chase down South. You couldn't get by without me, and compared to you, every other girl is a dead bore. What do you say?'

Rowan stopped and looked at him steadily. He was just

as attractive as he had ever been, but it had no effect on her. There was no apology for his carry-on with Sarah; she was expected to ignore it as always and just delight in the fact that he was over his bad mood. What a worm she had been!

'Sorry, Greg, I was deadly serious about finding my sister. I wish you could have shared the fun, but I do understand. I'll miss your friendship and I have no doubt you'll soon find a replacement for me in your life. I'd rather say goodbye now, so I'll hitch a ride with Debbie and Frank. See you.'

She grabbed up her things and ran over to the other car, feeling a sense of freedom that was incredible—like a butterfly that had shrugged off the hard restraining chrysalis and was floating beautiful and new, unencumbered. Would it last? Tonight, would she soak her pillow in bitter tears? She didn't think so. There was a certainty about her decision that went like sparkling wine coursing through her veins. Had she always felt restricted in her relationship with Greg? Had it been like an oppression of her own individuality to conform to his every wish? She must have been very thick not to have recognised it. But this new release of spirit, this exuberance, proved that it was true.

It also proved that she was immature and lacking in discernment. In future she would be very careful, especially about men. Marriage was out, for years and years. Perhaps in five years' time, or ten, she might have the wisdom to choose a partner for life, but until then she would steer clear of any deep attachment.

Her laughter ran out free and clear, startling the other two. She was going to enjoy herself, and avoid with great skill and dexterity those unbreakable cords of love her father spoke of. She would have no strings on her heart.

CHAPTER TWO

DIRECTLY across the street from where she stood, Rowan saw the Motueka Post Office, with the big clock pointing the time to five o'clock. It was to be her first call in this new town, to pick up mail and, if the staff were helpful, some information about accommodation. She had no doubts that they would be happy to advise her as long as they were not busy. Ever since she had arrived in Nelson six weeks ago, she had loved the South Island and the people she had met.

Coming from the big city of Auckland, she had marvelled at the ease with which she adopted the slower-paced, more friendly life-style of the sunshine centre of New Zealand. The first month she had stayed in Nelson itself, and had really enjoyed it. It was a city too, of course, with a beautiful cathedral dominating the commercial area, but in spite of the modern shops and thriving businesses, there was an almost leisurely village atmosphere where people had time to smile and talk to each other.

But she was no nearer finding her sister.

Rowan collected her mail and the information she wanted and walked slowly along the street towards her car, feeling the late February sunshine beating gloriously on her bare shoulders and arms.

Finding accommodation was not going to be easy. At the height of the holiday season all the motels and motor camps were full, as if the whole of New Zealand had zeroed in on this fantastic place, to relax in the sun and swim in the sparkling bays and clear rivers.

She didn't blame them, she would love a swim herself

right now, but she had to find somewhere to sleep, and not for just a night, but for a few weeks. She had thought Nelson small at first, but as her search had widened she discovered there were thousands more places she would have to visit.

Idly she stopped and looked into a bookshop window, more at her reflection than at the books. She had deliberately worn this pretty eye-catching sundress because of what the lady in the shop in Nelson had said last week.

'Buying another one of those, dear? It certainly suits you, but wouldn't you like a different shade?'

Rowan had been puzzled. 'This is the first time I've been in this shop.'

'But you were here yesterday. I'll swear to it. You bought exactly the same dress as you're holding now—same pattern, same style, same size. I'm positive.'

Excitement had bubbled up within Rowan because it was further proof that her sister did exist, and indeed visited the city. But she was no nearer finding her. The girl was not a regular customer and had paid cash.

Rowan felt even closer when it happened the second time in a café, where the waitress had insisted that she had already served her only five minutes before.

'You must have a double. People say we all have one, but this is extraordinary.'

But the worst time was when the garage attendant had been putting petrol into her car, and said, 'Got a new car, Jody?'

'I'm not Jody,' Rowan replied, her heart bursting with anticipation. 'Is she like me?'

'The spitting image. Go and have a look for yourself. She works in the Bank of New Zealand round the corner. Jody Spurr.'

And Rowan had almost run all the way to the Bank as soon as she could park her car. Breathlessly, she had searched the counters and when she saw the name plate with Jody Spurr on it and the girl behind it, she felt completely shattered. They both were slim with brown wavy hair, and were of medium height, but the likeness was purely superficial. It had been a body blow, and she wondered if the other two experiences been as false.

She had talked to the girl, explaining her quest, but Jody Spurr was not adopted, and that in itself was a relief. When she found her sister she wanted them to be alike in every way.

She was about to turn away from the bookshop when a light touch on her shoulder made her swing around, to find herself staring into the wickedest, most mischievous-looking hazel eyes she had ever seen. The man was tall and bronzed with a mop of unruly dark curls and he was smiling at her.

'Did anyone ever tell you that you were utterly beautiful?'

What a nerve! Rowan glared at him and said crushingly, 'Often, but with more charm.' She went to step past him.

'I'm going to kiss you!' He blocked her path with a mocking smile on his face.

'Oh, no, you're not,' Rowan said sharply, stepping back from him. 'I don't know what sort of drugs you're on, but go and hallucinate over someone else.'

He roared with laughter, and in one swift movement his arms imprisoned her and his mouth came down on hers for a surprisingly tender kiss.

Rowan jerked herself free and, outraged, slapped him hard on his very attractive face. 'Get lost. Keep away from me or I'll call the police!'

She rushed along the street, dived into the first shop she came to, and was pleased to find it was a restaurant. Shaking, she ordered a cup of tea and walked over to a spare table. The arrogant beast, thinking he could walk up to any strange girl on the street, and kiss her! She wiped her mouth vigorously. Nobody had kissed her since Greg, but that was not what upset her most. It had been his impudent manner.

She poured herself another cup of tea and put the crazy young man out of her mind, or tried to. She reached into her purse for her letters and it was only then she saw one in Greg's handwriting. That upset her all over again, so she thrust it back in her bag and opened the one from her parents. It was a lovely letter, full of encouragement and good suggestions. It was wonderful that they completely identified with her in this search. They would welcome her sister with open arms . . . when she found her. Much soothed, Rowan went back out into the sunshine and walked along to a seat situated under some large trees in front of an attractive church. Nervously, she glanced up and down the street, but relaxed as she saw no sign of the impudent young man. The street was thronged with holiday-makers and seasonal workers as well as shoppers.

'Would you accept an ice-cream as a token of appreciation, and also as a humble peace offering?'

In front of her stood her tormentor with a rakish grin on his cheerful face. Where had he come from?

'I would not,' Rowan answered furiously. 'If you don't stop making a nuisance of yourself, I *will* go to the police.'

'Don't tell me a super-looking chick like you has no sense of humour? I can't believe it. You won't let me stand here with the ice-cream melting all over the place, and refuse to forgive me?'

'Try me,' Rowan said through gritted teeth.

'It was a simple case of mistaken identity.'

'I don't believe you,' Rowan said flatly, her blue eyes flashing.

'Oh, but it's true. You're the image of my girl-friend. It's quite uncanny.'

'Huh! That's about as original as, "haven't we met

somewhere before?'' Or why don't you ask me if I come
here often?' She glanced along the street, trying to measure the distance to her car, and whether she could reach it
fast enough if he made a lunge for her. She wasn't really
frightened . . . more annoyed.

'I'm nothing if not original, lady. And if you'd hold
these damned ice-creams, I'll show you her photo, then
you'll be apologising to me.'

Rowan looked at him, then. Perhaps he was telling the
truth, but she doubted it. There was nothing humble
about him, nor apologetic. He stood there with a devil-
may-care grin on his face, waiting for her to accept the
ice-cream which was now dripping over his tanned hands.
She had to admit he had a certain charm, but she did not
believe his story.

Impatiently, she took the cones. 'Show me the photograph.'

His grin widened, then he carefully licked his fingers
with obvious enjoyment. 'Great ice-cream.' He wiped his
hands on a handkerchief, then slowly took a wallet from
the back pocket of his brief shorts. 'Eat yours before you
have to drink it.'

'Not before I see the photograph.'

'You're a hard woman. Sad to see someone so young, so
lacking in trust.' His greenish eyes were full of laughter.

'Get on with it,' Rowan said firmly.

He held a photograph a few inches away from her, and
her heart almost stopped beating. It was like looking at a
photo of herself.

'Who is she? What is her name? I want to meet her.'
The words came spilling out.

He ignored her and tucked the picture back in his
wallet, then took one of the ice-creams. 'Now that you've
found out I was telling the truth, perhaps you'll apologise.'

'Okay, I'm sorry, but it was an unlikely story.'

'Eat your ice-cream, then we'll talk, and you'll find I'm full of unlikely stories. I have a reputation for it.'

'I believe you.' Rowan licked her ice-cream, and battened down the desire to give him another swift smack on his charming face. She did not know what was warning her to proceed slowly, but there was a lithe animal-like wariness about the young man now, and she was uneasy. She had no doubt he knew her sister, but would he tell her where she could find her?

'Her name is Regan. What's yours?'

'Rowan.'

'Rowan.' He said it slowly and thoughtfully. 'You two could be twins. Like Romulus and Remus.'

Rowan sat silent. Again the vibrations warned her that this was a strange young man, even dangerous. He stood in front of her, barefooted, wearing the briefest of shorts, his bronzed, well-muscled body denoting health and strength and superb physical fitness. He was attractive and he knew it; there was a certain arrogance in his stance, and his eyes glinted down at her with thoughtful amusement.

'You really want to meet Regan?'

'Yes, I do.' Rowan tried to screen from him just how eager she was.

'I need something from you, Rowan. If you give it to me, I'll take you to Regan.'

'And if I don't give you what you want?' Rowan demanded, a little defiantly.

'Then I'll walk away and leave you.'

Rowan's eyes darted along the street as if hoping to see the girl walking towards them.

He laughed. 'You won't find her in this town. That's why I was so surprised to find you standing there on the street. Quite pleasantly surprised, if I may say so.'

'You say she's your girl-friend.' Rowan felt a blush colour her cheeks as she remembered his kiss and was irritated. 'If you walk away, I'll just go on until I find her myself, and I can tell you she won't be pleased with you for not helping me.'

'I have certain ways of making Regan pleased with me, even when she's angry.'

Rowan glared up at him indignantly, yet even as she met his dancing, mischievous hazel eyes she felt herself grin. He was telling the truth again. Her sister would find it impossible to stay angry very long with him—he really was a charmer.

'What do I have to do?' she asked, defeated.

'You have to go out with me tonight to a dinner-dance, and pretend you're Regan. You'll have fun, I promise you, but not as much as I will.'

'Where is it being held?' Rowan asked warily.

'Ah! You're trying to wrest information from me which you are not entitled to. I want your promise that you will do what I ask. You see, Regan promised me she would meet me here, but something came up and she couldn't make it. It's important that she partners me tonight, and she will be quite pleased that you helped me out of my predicament.'

Rowan stared thoughtfully at him. Every sense in her was screaming caution, yet there was no harm that she could see in filling in for her sister. Or was there? 'If I agree, would you let me speak to Regan on the phone? I'd like to clear it with her.'

His greeny eyes were filled with malicious amusement as if he knew her problem, her lack of trust. 'Sorry, she can't be reached by phone until tomorrow. You'll have to trust me.'

But that was just what she didn't do. 'If I go to this dance, you will tell me how to get hold of her?'

'Cross my heart,' he said with a laugh. 'But before you take it on, I want your word that you will not let anyone guess you're not Regan.'

'But I don't know anything about her,' Rowan protested. 'Where does she work? What are her tastes? I might muck it up.'

'I wouldn't do that if I were you.' There was a cruel light in his eyes. 'Regan will be put right out of your reach for good if you cross me.' Then he was smiling confidently again. 'You're intelligent, and I'll be with you; we'll pull the wool right over their eyes. Look on it as a challenge.'

Her heart was filled with misgiving. There was something very peculiar about the whole thing. Yet, she was so close to finding her sister, and if this young man walked away, it might take her months to find Regan.

'My name is Jordan Hewitt. I come from a highly respectable family. You won't come to any harm with me and, as I said before, you'll really enjoy yourself. When I put on my glad rags you'll find yourself the envy of every woman in the room. They'll hate your guts for having the best-looking, wittiest, and most charming escort.'

'I bet there'll be no one there to match you for modesty, either,' Rowan retorted smartly, but she had to smile.

Jordan laughed, his eyes dancing. 'You look so like Regan, yet you are incredibly different. Like sweet and sour pickles, or lemon meringue pie, or vinegar on fish and chips. I like a little spice in a girl.'

'Am I really so like her?' Rowan longed to know.

'The living image, especially in that dress. She bought one just like it a couple of weeks ago.'

So it *had* been her in that shop in Nelson. Rowan felt a great welling of love for Regan . . . they even liked the same clothes. She had to meet her. 'Okay, I'll do it. I'll go to this dance with you.'

'Great. And you'll give me your word that no matter what happens or what people say to you, you will not tell them you're not Regan.'

'Yes, I'll give you my word.' Rowan thought that if anything happened against Regan's best interests, she could always go round the next day and explain what had happened.

Triumph blazed in Jordan's eyes. 'And, of course, you are the sort to whom a promise is sacred?'

'Yes,' Rowan said firmly. 'Having given my word, I won't break it.'

'That's great. I'm exactly the opposite, an incorrigible liar—it's half my charm.'

'I don't find it charming,' Rowan said disapprovingly.

'You will,' Jordan smiled with smug assurance. 'Now tell me something about yourself. Where do you come from? What are doing down here? Where are you staying? How are you travelling?'

'I come from Auckland,' Rowan said carefully, deciding suddenly that she was not going to tell him everything. 'I'm here on holiday. I have nowhere to stay yet, and that's my Mazda over there—the red one.'

'Whew! I smell money. Who's bankrolling you?'

Rowan gave him a withering glance. 'My parents gave me the car and the holiday. Is money all-important to you?'

'No. I've got plenty of my own, but it's always nice to know where there's more. Regan's got none.'

'That shouldn't make a difference to how you feel about her,' Rowan replied acidly.

He grinned wickedly, 'It doesn't, but it could make a difference about how I feel about you.'

'Forget it,' Rowan said caustically as she stood up. 'You and I have nothing in common. I don't even like you.'

'That could change.' He was laughing at her.

'I wouldn't hold your breath,' she returned grimly, and stooped to pick up her letters which had spilled to the ground. She wished she hadn't got involved in this charade.

'Don't be mad at me, Rowan. I'm very sorry I teased you. Let's be friends.'

'I think you're a rogue.' She stood very straight and eyed him steadily. In spite of herself she felt her lips curving into a smile. He really was a fascinating man; no wonder Regan had fallen for him. Rowan only hoped her sister knew what she was doing, and was strong enough to handle such an overpowering personality.

'I am, a rogue and a rascal, and a vagabond, everybody says so. I am the black sheep of the family, a disgrace to the district. I drink, I gamble, I don't do an honest day's work, and I am a thorn in the side of my painfully honest and upright brother.'

'I believe every word of it,' Rowan said forthrightly. 'But why does Regan love you? She should have more sense.'

'She thinks she can change me, be a good influence on me. Do you think you could be a good influence on me, Rowan?'

'I wouldn't waste my time,' Rowan answered with devastating honesty.

'Oh, Drew would *approve* of you,' Jordan told her in tones that made the statement sound like an insult.

'Who's he?'

'My big brother. He is honest, hardworking, a good farmer, and a leader in the community—and terribly, terribly dull.'

'Poor man,' Rowan said lightly, a bit shaken by the malice in Jordan's voice. 'Are you going to tell me where the dance is? I'd better start trying to find a bed for the night.'

'You could always share mine,' Jordan offered impudently.

'No, thank you. Have you any other suggestions, bright or otherwise?'

Again he threw back his head and laughed. 'I could go for you in a big way, Rowan. You've no idea how funny it is to hear you take chunks out of me, when Regan treats me with such loving kindness. She's never nasty.'

Rowan's eyes softened. 'Is she really nice?'

'Yes, she is gentle, sweet, and very beautiful . . . and I love her very much.'

For once Jordan was not laughing and Rowan felt he was being honest for the first time since she had met him. 'You love her very much but you still mistook me for her?'

'Only for a moment. It was the dress that fooled me.'

'You mean you knew before you kissed me?' Rowan demanded angrily.

'Of course. But the temptation was too much for me.'

'I'm *glad* I hit you.' She turned and stalked across the street and unlocked her car, so furious that she bungled it, then dropped the keys.

Jordan swooped on them. 'I'll drive. It would be dangerous to get behind a wheel in your condition. And anyway, you don't know where we're going.'

For a moment Rowan wanted to shout that she wouldn't go anywhere with him. He was a menace, and even the thought of finding Regan began to pale, if it meant staying with him. But she had promised, so she swallowed her anger and walked around to the passenger's side in silence.

He flung the door open with a devastating grin. 'That's my girl. Hop in. We're going right over the top of that mountain, Marble Mountain, but more commonly called Takaka Hill. You haven't been there yet, have you?'

'No,' Rowan said shortly, getting in and closing the door. 'Where's your car?'

'In the garage. I pranged it last week, but I'll be more careful with this sporty model.'

'You'd better be,' Rowan muttered, feeling the circumstances were getting out of control. She was letting an unknown young man drive her to an unknown destination, and the longer she was in his company the less she trusted him.

Jordan started the car and eased out into the traffic. 'Don't sulk now, you'll spoil the trip. This drive is really spectacular. We go through Riwaka first, you'll see the hops hung from wires and the tobacco plants all leafy and green, then we'll start over the hill. We'll climb nine miles up one side, winding all the way, from sea level to the highest point, 2,595 feet, then abruptly down the other side for six miles to Takaka again at sea level. Hope you don't suffer from car sickness.'

'I don't. Well, not with a good driver.'

'You wound me, Rowan. I'm an excellent driver, and as the tourist verbiage would have it, this fascinating drive will never be forgotten. It only takes about an hour, but years ago it was a full day's walk. One lone traveller got lost and his bleached bones weren't found until years later.'

Rowan believed him. The ascent was so steep it took her breath away, and as Jordan concentrated on his gears and driving, the handkerchief-sized fields were soon lost from sight. The green tail of the valley trailed away below, seen down lurching cliffs, through fine screens of tiny-leafed manuka and native forest, and plantings of exotic pines, laced with ferns and flowers, and thick summer grasses.

As corner after corner came up gaspingly fast she could only marvel at the variety and beauty of the scenery, the panoramic views of Motueka spread out before them when Jordan swung on to a prominence to give her a more leisurely look over the vast sweep of the whole Tasman Bay right through to Nelson, sparkling and brilliant in the late afternoon sunshine. Then climbing on and on, to see weird and wonderfully-shaped boulders strewn across the hillside, sculptured by the weather into art works.

'Golden Bay Boundary. Now we'll descend and this is the best part, driving through native bush tunnels and seeing Takaka Valley below. There's the Tasman Mountains over there. How long are you planning to stay? I'd love to show you around. We've got everything here in Golden Bay.'

'If I could get a place to stay, I might take you up on that. I could possibly stay a month. In Motueka, they said all the small cottages were in use for the apple-picking season. There was just nothing.'

Jordan flashed her a cheerful grin. 'I know the very place for you. It's an old house, high on the hill above Collingwood—fabulous views. You'd love it. Passionfruit growing in the garden, high-ceilinged rooms and cool for the summer, secluded, big verandahs for sunbathing; how does it strike you?'

'Fantastic. You mean it's free now? How much is the rent?'

'It will be very low rent, and I can take you straight there. Friends of mine were there and they left only yesterday, so I know it's still vacant. If you were living there, I could take you all over the place, swimming, fishing, gold panning.'

'Don't you work at all?' Rowan pulled her glance away from the incredibly beautiful valley below to stare at Jordan.

'Never. Work is a dirty four-letter word as far as I'm concerned. All work and no play makes Jack a dull boy, they say, so I just cut out work entirely, and my life is anything but dull.'

'Where do you get your money from, if it's not too personal a question?'

'Oh, I don't mind telling you. When my father died he left the farm carefully tied up between my mother and Drew and myself. We all get a third of the income, but only Drew works. The theory was we'd work in partnership, but I get the same amount whether I work or not.'

'That's terrible. What does Drew think of the arrangement?'

'It would take too long to describe my dear sanctimonious brother's idea on the situation, but I'm sure he loves it. The district thinks he's wonderful to put up with two drones on his back, and he stands up well under all the praise.'

'My sympathy is all with him,' Rowan said sternly.

'So is everyone's,' Jordan grinned wickedly. 'At least I keep out of his way; Mother keeps on his back. You'll have to come and visit our happy home.'

'I'd rather not, thank you. Surely it doesn't have to be like that. Why does he put up with it?'

'He has no choice unless he sells the farm and we all share the proceeds. That's what Mother wants, but I don't care either way. I plan my own life-style.'

'Why doesn't he sell?' Rowan didn't know why she was interested in Drew, probably because she wasn't all that keen on Jordan.

'Drew sell? You've got to be joking! He loves the farm, he loves Collingwood, he'd sooner be *dead* than live anywhere else. Most people over here feel that way. It's more an idea in the mind than actual geographic position. Don't get hooked or you'll never want to leave—it gets into your blood. Some kids grow up here, leave for other parts of New Zealand and when they've established themselves in good jobs and fine homes, suddenly jack it all in and come back to the Bay, even if they have to work on the roads.'

'And you? Do you have the same feeling for the place?' Rowan asked, full of curiosity.

'You bet. I'll never leave.'

'Poor Drew.'

'Poor Drew indeed. But don't worry for him, he's a great big strapping fellow, well able to look after himself.'

Rowan doubted it. If Jordan's mother was anything like her younger son, Drew would have plenty of problems.

All the way over, Jordan had pointed out interesting places that he would take her to, the Limestone Caves at Ngarua, the Pupu Springs near Takaka, the tame eels at Anatoki, the Cobb Dam, and mentioned the Heaphy Track which she had heard was one of the most beautiful walks in the country. But she decided to reserve her decision to go anywhere with him until after she met Regan. If Regan was to go with him, she would accept his invitations, but if she wasn't, then Rowan would think twice about being so much in his company.

'Have you got a real sexy dress in those bags you're carrying? I want you to wear something real classy. I'd like to stand this lot on their ears.'

Rowan smiled as she thought of her red dress with the plunging neckline that her father had declared made him blush even though he was a doctor. It wasn't her favourite, but it was quite extravagant. 'Yes, I've got a very stylish gown that might suit. Why do you want to upset these people? Have they done you any harm?'

'They're so smug and self-satisfied it will do them good to be shaken up. I've built myself a bit of a reputation as a hell-raiser round here and they reckon I couldn't get a decent girl to go out with me. They took bets on it.'

'But I thought Regan was your girl-friend. Don't they think she's a lady?'

'Of course they do,' he said impatiently. 'But Regan and I have to be careful. Her father is a straight-laced, religious kook and he won't let her go out with me. She's allowed to go out with Drew, of course.'

'But if you're careful about keeping your relationship quiet, why drag me along tonight?' Rowan demanded.

'Oh, Regan and I thought it was time we came out in the open. It was to be tonight, and she's just sick she can't make it. I was too. She knew I'd told everyone I was bringing someone special to the dance and she felt she was letting me down. She was twenty last month, and she and

I both thought it was time her father stopped being so protective.'

Joy flared in Rowan's heart. That was further proof that Regan was her twin. She would put up with anything now to meet her.

'We're nearly into Collingwood now. It's only a little town, really tucked into the curve of the Bay. I'll take you straight up to the house and fix up the details later. That's the Hospital on the left, we turn right to the township, or left to our farm from here.

They travelled beside the Bay for a short distance, and in the gathering dusk Rowan caught just a glimpse of the lovely smooth water and bush-clad hills, and fishing boats tied at the jetty, before Jordan swung right off the main road and changed down to charge up a very steep gravel road.

'You're home,' he announced as he reversed the Mazda into a big double garage cut into the steep hillside.

'There's not much room to drive out,' Rowan said a little nervously. 'And are you sure the owners won't mind?'

'Positive. I'll ring them now. First I'll give you a hand to unload.'

Before she had time to protest further he was unloading the boot and she grabbed a few things and followed him down the cement steps and through a doorway into a large kitchen.

'Have a scout round while I ring Kevin,' Jordan said as he walked to the phone.

Rowan stood nervously by her cases. She wasn't going to wander through anyone's house until she was satisfied they wanted her there. She had thought he had described it as an old house, but the kitchen was beautifully modern, with floor-to-ceiling cupboards along one side, and large windows facing on to a hillside of native bush, so close she thought she could touch it.

'Thanks, Kev, I knew it would be okay. Sure, she's a fine girl, responsible and all that . . . I've known her for years.'

As he hung up Rowan gasped, 'You lied to him. You've only known me a couple of hours.'

Jordan grinned wickedly, 'I warned you that I'm an incorrigible liar, you just didn't believe me. The place is yours for a month. Put the kettle on and I'll nip down to the store for some goodies for you.'

'I'll go with you. I'd rather do my own shopping.'

'No, you don't. You're not to be seen until you enter the hall with me. I'll be back in five minutes.'

He disappeared and she felt again a strange panic that warned her she was being stupid to let him organise her life to suit himself. But it was only for this one night, then tomorrow she would meet Regan. Sighing, she walked through to the next room, and found herself in a pleasant high-ceilinged living room with an open archway to the lounge. Both rooms were simply but comfortably furnished and she wandered to the window at the far end and stared down at the dark water of the Bay. The single string of street lights were shining and being reflected in the mirror surface, and a lighted fishing launch came into view and throbbed noisily up the narrow channel to its berth.

Yes, she could be happy here for a month, there was a warmth about this house that was more than the leftover heat trapped from a hot summer's day. Perhaps she was being fanciful, but there was an atmosphere of a house which had been loved, that these walls had sheltered and protected happy and contented people.

She tried to shrug off the feeling of impending disaster and walked determinedly into the wide old-fashioned passage, peeping hastily into the two bedrooms, and then finished the circuit by checking the attractive modern bathroom-washhouse complex and returning to the kitchen.

She heard the roar of the Mazda take the hill and saw the lights flash on the dark trees as Jordan reversed into the garage.

'Here's all you need to sustain life until tomorrow.' Jordan briskly strode in and dropped a cardboard carton on the freestanding breakfast nook. 'You'll find a linen cupboard in the passage, so sort yourself out, and I'll be back at eight to pick you up.'

'Where are you going?'

'Home to get my best glad rags on. I'll take your car. For Pete's sake get that mournful look off your face. I'm taking you to a party, not a funeral. See you in an hour.'

It was all right for him to be cheerful, everything was going according to *his* plan. She had to shake off this mood. She was supposed to be Regan and she thought if her sister was going out in public with the man she loved, breaking new territory, and defying restrictions for the first time, she would be wildly excited and deliriously happy. Rowan decided she would have to do a mental leap-frog over tonight's doings, and think only of the excitement of meeting Regan next day.

Unconsciously her lips curved into a smile. There was no need to pretend—tomorrow she would be talking to her other half. She sang as she found the sheets and pillowslips and made up the front bedroom, and she sang as she showered and washed her hair. As she used the blow-dryer on her hair she concentrated on what they would say to each other, and by the time she had dressed and completed her make-up, she felt she was doing Regan justice.

Jordan whistled when he saw her. 'Smashing! You're sensational. What a dress, what a figure! I always knew how Regan would look if she ever had money to dress properly. Nobody could tell you apart, you've got my word on that. Nobody but me.'

'How can you tell?'

'That's my secret.' Jordan winked teasingly. 'How about a kiss to start the evening off on the right foot? You're going to be my sister-in-law someday.'

Rowan moved with a swirl of her red chiffon skirts. 'Keep away from me! If you attempt to maul me, I'll blow this crazy pretence sky-high. Understand?'

The devil-may-care grin on his attractive face showed he wasn't one whit ashamed of his outrageous suggestion. 'You enjoyed it the first time and so did I. Never mind, turn around so that I can view you from every aspect. Stop glaring, this is business. Will that dress stay together when you dance?'

Nervously, Rowan touched her bare shoulders, and the swathe of soft chiffon which moulded her breasts cunningly and clung to her slender waist then fell in floating panels around her legs like petals of some exotic flower. 'Is it too much? Greg chose it for me when we entered a disco-dancing competition. He said I needed something flamboyant to catch the judge's eye. It was okay in an Auckland night-club, but please say if it's not suitable for a country-style dance.'

'Spin round,' Jordan ordered.

'I've got plenty of others.' Rowan was almost pleading now, convinced she had made a mistake.

Imperiously, Jordan waved his hand again, his greeny eyes bright and hard.

Rowan spun round, knowing her dress would flare out waist high making her legs look extravagantly long and the soft scarf which fell from her shoulders would float away leaving her back bare.

'Stupendous. A modern miracle of construction.' He clapped his hands in approval. 'Grab a wrap and we'll be off. I just can't wait to see their faces drop. You're really going to bowl them over. Regan will appreciate what you're doing for her, that's a promise. But you remember you *are* Regan. If anyone asks you where you got the dress,

say you borrowed it. She couldn't afford a creation like
that. Remember also to keep a guard on that acid tongue
of yours. Regan is a shy little darling, so if anyone asks you
something you can't answer, look wistful and shy and
stammer a bit. Can you blush?'

'Not to order,' Rowan snapped.

'If the occasion demands it, I'll guarantee to say something to make you blush without any effort at all.'

'I don't see what Regan sees in you,' Rowan said
furiously, picking up her cobweb-soft woollen shawl and
clutchbag and following him out to the garage. 'She must
be mentally deficient.'

She heard him chuckle in the darkness as he held the car
door open. 'I'll give you a free demonstration of my
charms when this evening is over, then you may be in the
position to judge more clearly.'

Seething, Rowan tried to think of a suitably crushing
remark as they drove down the hill. They turned right at
the garage and left into the main street. She noted the
distance carefully and was relieved to think if the going
became too rough she could easily walk out and return
home in a matter of minutes. Cars lined both sides of the
street so it was dearly going to be a big gathering.

She took Jordan's proffered arm as they walked towards
the well-lit Memorial Hall and she had to admit he was a
very handsome young man.

The dinner was fabulous, and seated with Jordan
amongst a group of his friends, she soon found the initial
nervousness wearing off. There had been a stunned
silence when they first took their places, but apart from a
few sly digs at Jordan, they accepted her without hesitation and were soon talking and laughing in high good
spirits. Jordan was quick to handle any awkward question
and steer the conversation away from her, and she had no
trouble gazing at him in admiration. He was a charming
and stimulating dinner companion and very protective of

her, while the wicked sparkle in his eyes told her he was enjoying himself immensely.

When the tables were cleared away and the dancing began she soon found he was a superb dancer, and she had no trouble matching her steps to his. He refused to let her dance with anyone else, for which she was grateful, and his obvious possessiveness made the others laugh and jeer at him.

'Enjoying yourself, Rowan?' His alert hazel eyes smiled down at her.

'I really am.' Her vivacious face and sparkling eyes showed it to be the truth. 'They just accept I'm Regan. It's been a breeze, and I don't know what I was so scared about. The band is great, too.'

'Yes, they're the best. Wait till after supper, they'll really start swinging. Do you enjoy dancing?'

'Yes, I do. Greg and I took lessons together. We got as far as a Silver Medal apiece before we gave it up.'

'You've mentioned this Greg several times this evening. Is he special in your life?'

Rowan looked away. She felt guilty that she hadn't even read the letter from Greg which she had picked up at the Post Office. Poor Greg, he would never believe that she had got over him so completely that she could ignore the first letter he had written her. But it might be safer for her if Jordan thought she had someone steady. 'You could say that.'

'Lucky chap,' Jordan commented cheerfully. 'Still, I'm glad he's not here tonight. He mightn't be too keen on my monopolising all your time.'

Rowan giggled. 'That's the understatement of the year. Greg brooks no competition.'

Jordan pulled her closer, his hazel eyes glinting devilishly. 'And I'm big competition in anybody's language. Go on, admit it.'

Rowan laughed, 'I hate to dent your colossal ego, but

my heart beats no faster because I'm dancing with you.'

'Cheeky. I could change that if I had a mind to, but tonight, you are doing a perfect job covering for Regan so I won't move up into overdrive with you. I suppose you realise that, apart from the bridal couple, you're the sole topic of conversation here tonight.'

She lifted puzzled blue eyes to meet his gaze. 'I haven't noticed a thing.'

'I know that. That's what is so beautiful. You're acting so naturally that it's making the whole thing even more hilarious. I know everyone in this Hall and you've blown their minds. They look, and look away, not believing what they're seeing.'

'But I'm not doing anything unusual,' Rowan protested.

Jordan roared with laughter. 'The fact that you are out with me is enough to keep their tongues wagging in disapproval for months. The fact that you're dancing and doing it well has amazed them. Just go on enjoying yourself and I'll keep you well clear of the front line.'

After supper the beat of the band warmed up and most of the older couples were content to sit and talk and leave the floor to the younger people.

Jordan had been drinking steadily, but not more than any others in the party, but Rowan had been carefully limiting her drinks. She felt the situation demanded a clear and unclouded mind. Still, she could hardly refuse when Jordan brought her a long glass of punch. She had only sipped half a glass when he had her on her feet again and she was glad because it tasted fairly potent.

'Right, girlie, here is where we show them a few extras.' Jordan began weaving some intricate steps in time with the quickened tempo of the band and Rowan had no trouble in following him. He danced very like Greg, and as she spun and twisted she laughed at him, enjoying the rhythm and beat which throbbed through her.

She didn't know when the floor cleared and people started to clap, but when she became aware of it she wanted to stop. She had no intention of making an exhibition of herself, but something was happening she could not control. It was almost as if Jordan was mesmerising her with those wicked eyes of his and she was almost part of him, dancing above her usual self, carried on by the chanting and clapping of the crowd, her skirt flaring out, her scarf and hair flying and her high-heeled shoes moving of their own volition. It was a frightening experience as he flung her one way, then the next, catching her expertly and holding her high above his head as he whirled like a dervish, dropping her back to earth without losing a step. She knew she was dancing better than she had ever danced in her life and exhilaration swamped the fear and she forgot the crowd and became one with the music and the dance.

Jordan caught her in his arms and carried her off the floor in triumph as the crowd applauded them.

She was dimly aware that the dance floor was crowded again, and shakily reached for her drink to quench her parched throat. Jordan left her alone at the table and returned with another ice-cold drink.

'You deserve that, honey. Boy, that was really something. There's not a man in the room who wouldn't slit my throat to possess you, Rowan, and look at the women!' He walked away again and she was glad. She could hardly focus on his face and her legs felt rubbery. What had possessed her to dance like that? She felt utterly humiliated. The faces she could see across the room didn't seem envious. The women's eyes slid away from her gaze and she wanted to rush out of the Hall and hide.

'Enjoying yourself, Regan?'

Rowan wished the room would stop spinning so that she could focus on the owner of that deep, fiercely sharp voice.

'Of course,' she mumbled stupidly, wishing the man would go away, or that Jordan would come back.

'Look at me, Regan.' His voice crackled with authority.

Rowan decided to ignore him. Propping her hand under her chin to steady it, she reached out for her drink with what she hoped was casual nonchalance.

'You're drunk. I'm disgusted with you.' A hand moved the drink out of her reach.

'I think you're a bit disgusting yourself,' Rowan managed to enunciate with great care, then spoiled it by giggling.

Strong, tanned fingers grasped her chin and forced her head up, and her shocked blue eyes encountered a pair of intense grey eyes glaring furiously down at her. 'You didn't expect to see me here tonight, did you, Regan?'

'No, I didn't.' He was a big man, well over six feet, broad-shouldered, slim-hipped and extremely good-looking, apart from the angry scowl. 'You're hurting me,' she said plaintively.

He let her go and impatiently pulled out a chair beside her and sat down. 'Tell me, Regan, just tell me what you hoped to gain from this performance? I just can't believe it. You've blown two years' effort by coming here tonight. And to get drunk . . .'

'I'm not drunk. This is my first drink tonight . . . almost . . .' She was appalled to hear the words come out thick and slow, and the disbelieving expression on his face made her giggle even though she knew this was no laughing matter. Who was he? Why didn't Jordan come back and rescue her? Her brain was functioning all right, but her speech was definitely off and her head, legs and arms also felt heavy and unmanageable.

His eyes narrowed thoughtfully as he reached for her drink and took one sip then another, then slapped the table with the flat of his hand as he said explosively, '*Jordan, it's got to be Jordan.* He's doctored your drink. How could you be so stupid? You're an absolute idiot!'

Silently Rowan agreed. She had been abysmally stupid. She knew she shouldn't have trusted Jordan—her instinct had told her that. And she had also obviously hurt Regan. This big angry man had said she had blown two years' effort by coming here tonight, and her big blue eyes filled with tears which slid slowly down her cheeks.

'Stop that. Pull yourself together. So far, I'm the only one who knows you're bombed out of your mind. If your father hears about this . . .' He stood up hastily. 'We might save your reputation yet. You're going to dance with me . . .'

'Not . . . can't . . . stand.' Rowan gestured helplessly at him, pleading for him to understand.

'Oh, but you're going to stand, my dear,' he gritted savagely. 'And you're going to gracefully circle this damned room twice, and you'll smile as if you were enjoying it, that way people just may think I asked Jordan to escort you here and partner you until I arrived. But they'd have to be a bit crazy to think I'd let Jordan partner anyone I cared for.'

Rowan felt herself being pulled on to her feet and clung instinctively to the lapels of his jacket. She felt his arms go around her like steel bands and he started to move with the music.

'Smile, darn you, smile. I won't let you fall, and the floor is crowded enough so that people will not notice that you're dragging your feet with all the grace of a rag doll.'

Rowan thought that on a short list of people she disliked most, this arrogant brute would lead at a gallop. Who was he? Regan's boy-friend? Fiancé? Husband? Anything was possible.

'Hello, Drew, old chap. Splendid that you could get back for the dance. I said to Margie that Regan would not be here if you weren't in the offing. How did the trip go?'

'Fine, just fine, Bill. Being election year, politicians

seem unbelievably helpful. I'll tell you all about it tomorrow, I'm tired tonight. Regan and I won't be staying late.'

The first circuit of the dance floor was painfully difficult, and it felt as if they had travelled five hundred miles over difficult terrain, but the second time around they seemed to get into some sort of rhythm and it became almost enjoyable. Regan had no trouble smiling as one couple after another greeted Drew warmly, and smiled at her affectionately. My, but he was popular, this tall stranger; people really warmed to him. And she was included into this charmed fellowship because she was his friend. When she had been dancing with Jordan people had not wanted to meet her eyes, they had hastily looked elsewhere, but she knew now that their expression had been concern and anxiety. Oh, golly, what had she done to Regan?

'Drew.' In her surprise she spoke his name out loud.

'Yes, Regan, what is it?' His dark head bent politely towards her, his expression kindly and encouraging. 'You're doing fine.'

Her blue eyes filled unexpectedly with tears and she dropped her head against his shoulder so that he could not see her dismay. Now she knew who he was. He was Drew Hewitt, Jordan's brother. The one who did all the work and was admired by the whole district ... what had Jordan said about him? Oh, yes, a strapping big fellow, well able to take care of himself. Well, that was correct at any rate. And he would also be well able to take care of the girl he loved. Did he love Regan? Did she love him? Was this whole stupid idea a plan to wreck their happiness? And she had made it all possible. Oh, if only she were dead.

'Hang in there, mate, we're almost to the door.'

She realised that in dancing so close to him, almost like a second skin, her despair must have been obvious to him, and she was grateful for his encouraging words and the soothing touch of his hand on her back which stroked her firmly yet tenderly, almost like the way a rider gentles a nervous horse . . . and it worked, she felt incredibly safe and protected in his arms, and for one crazy moment she envied Regan with all her heart.

As he passed her table Drew flicked her shawl from the chair and as he reached the door, solicitously wrapped it about her bare shoulders as he briefly explained to yet another friend that they were off to the Post Office to get his mail before going home.

CHAPTER THREE

OUTSIDE the Hall, Drew half carried, half dragged her to an opulent looking station-wagon and poured her on to the front seat. She felt about as graceful as a bag of chaff, and was humiliated that he had to bend down and put her feet in, one at a time, before he could shut the door.

As he slid into the driver's seat he said sharply, 'Sit up, Regan. Jeff's heading this way.'

Rowan giggled helplessly. She was absolutely incapable of moving hand or foot, and the sight of his angry face seemed hilariously funny.

Grabbing her roughly, he straightened her against the seat and put his arm about her to stop her sliding sideways. 'If you don't stop laughing, I'll treat you as I would any hysterical female and smack your face. I mean it.'

She bit her lip fiercely, trying to obey, but her large blue eyes brimmed with laughter as she gazed into his furious grey ones.

'You two seem to be having fun. Is it a private joke or can you share it with me?'

'It's private,' Drew said firmly and jerked Rowan towards him so roughly that she was nearly winded. She gasped for air then buried her face in his shoulder trying to muffle her laughter. She knew it wasn't funny, she knew by the hard tautness of his body against hers that he could have cheerfully killed her, but she couldn't stop laughing.

'Dad was saying you made a real killing up North, Drew. He's full of admiration for the way you led the delegation to Parliament, said you'd missed your calling. Not only did you make them back-up, but they went over backwards trying to accommodate you. The district will be more than grateful for what you have achieved.'

'It was nothing, Jeff. Election year always opens the Public Purse, you know that.'

'You timed it just right, Dad said. In another few months the queue would have been too long to give you that individual treatment. You did well. And so did you, Regan. Boy, I didn't know you could dance like that. Hey, Drew, you can't take her home yet. Jordan wouldn't let any of us dance with her.'

'He was taking good care of her for me,' Drew said smoothly. He switched on the motor. 'Sorry to disappoint you, Jeff, but I've had it, so we're going to pick up the mail and head home.'

As he removed his arm and drove down the street, Rowan slid half off the seat on to the floor.

'That's the best place for you,' Drew said savagely. 'You can stay down there until I collect the mail.'

Rowan heard the car door slam. As if she had any option! She had to stay on the floor because her legs were hopeless. What had Jordan put in her drink? Wait till she caught up with him!

Drew was back, flinging a pile of mail on the back seat before he drove off. 'What am I to do with you, Regan? I can't take you home in this condition. Your father would go berserk. And who could blame him? If I had Jordan here, you wouldn't be the only one who couldn't walk, believe me.'

As the car braked suddenly, Rowan sprawled in an ungainly heap. She couldn't understand what had happened any more than Drew could. But it was worse for her, she could hear everything he said but couldn't speak, although her mind seemed quite alert.

The passenger door opened and Drew bent down and lifted her out. 'Sorry about the rough treatment, Regan. Look, try and stand up. Help me, so that I can help you.

I've brought you down the back road to the beach. If you can walk off the effects of the drink, we just might be able to get you back into your bedroom without your father being any the wiser.'

'Can't,' Rowan mumbled, and slid down on to the sand.

'Oh, yes, you *can* do it.' Drew hefted her on to her feet and pulled her arm around his shoulders and half carried, half dragged her half a mile along the beach, then turned and went back to the car with her. Breathing heavily he propped her against the bonnet.

'You're worse, not better. The fresh air has hit you and it will be hours before you're in any shape to move. I'm not taking you home where Jordan can get at you.'

Rowan stare back at him owlishly.

He gave an exasperated sigh. 'How could you do this, Regan? I can't believe you'd be such a fool as to trust Jordan. But you must have. You've not got a dress like that. Where did you get it? Did Jordan buy it for you? You look like a high-class call-girl.'

'You should know.' Rowan was startled to find her voice loud and clear.

Drew looked at her sharply. 'Are you having me on?'

Solemnly she shook her head, her luminous eyes sad and mournful, then a tear ran down her cheek and she sniffed inelegantly.

'Okay, okay,' he muttered impatiently, pulling a handkerchief from his pocket, and wiping her eyes. 'Blow.'

She was suddenly laughing again. Fancy having a stranger helping you blow your nose, but her hands were as useless as her legs.

Drew stared down at her. 'We'll just wait for a bit. I wish I knew what he'd fed you. It could be cocaine, although I don't think even Jordan would be so foolish. One trip on that stuff can have distressing side-effects, especially being taken by someone like you who has never even tasted alcohol. I don't think he would hurt you, he loves you too much to do you a permanent injury. Why, oh why, Regan? You had it all in your hand. Why blow the whole thing with this caper?'

Rowan looked out across the water of the Bay. She had upset Regan's plans in some terrible way. Golly, she felt rotten. If only she could be sick she might get rid of the effect of the drug. Drew might be mad at her, but he couldn't be as angry with her as she was with herself. She had walked right into Jordan's plan with her eyes wide open. If she had been in Auckland, she would never have gone out with a stranger, especially someone as obviously wicked as Jordan. And if she had been in strange company, she would not have accepted a drink except directly from a qualified barman.

She knew all about drugs. She had been to plenty of parties with Greg where they had been freely available, but in those circumstances she had stuck to lemonade and made sure she chose her own unopened can, too. Why had she been so naïve and trusting? Just because it was a small country village and she thought Jordan cared for Regan, she had let herself be fooled. She should have been more cautious. Drugs were everywhere . . .

'Try and walk now. See if you're any better,' he coaxed. 'Come on.' He took her arm encouragingly.

She grimly tried to concentrate on moving her legs, but nothing happened. He supported her with his arm and moved her forwards, but she just fell against him.

Picking her up, he put her back in the car. 'I'm going to book you in at the motor camp. You'll be safe there and I'll come back in the morning after you've had a few hours' sleep.'

He drove a short distance back up the road then stopped the car. He disappeared in the darkness and after a while returned, then drove on to the motor camp, parked and picked her up. He dropped her on a bunk in a small cabin and bent to straighten her dress, but it defied him and, exasperated, he flung a rug over her, tucking her into its folds until only her head and hands were showing.

'There, now you look like my little mate. When I saw you dancing like that, it was as if I'd never known you. No wonder the men stared, you were enough to stir any man. How could a mere dress change you so? And where did you learn to dance like that? That was purely professional . . . has Jordan been teaching you on the side?'

Rowan blinked her long lashes desperately. She wanted to ask him what she had done to hurt Regan, but no words would come. She shook her head despairingly.

Drew's expression changed to one of compassion and he took her hand in his. 'Look, kid, you'll be okay soon. I'll go and find Jordan and see what he doped you with, and maybe we can speed up your recovery. Thank God I came home on the early ferry to Picton. I only caught it by the skin of my teeth. I've never felt like using brute force on Jordan before, but this time he's gone too far. How did he trick you? I can't believe that you would throw everything away for one night out with him.'

Tears of frustrated rage slid down Rowan's cheeks. Why had she followed Jordan like a gullible fool? Drew wasn't the only one who would like to use a bit of physical violence on Jordan.

Again Drew wiped her eyes. 'You must have gone willingly. Even Jordan is incapable of dressing you in that gear and bringing you along by force. There's no use crying your eyes out now. It will be time enough when your father finds out, and that won't be long. Some kindly soul will inform him before the night's out, or by daybreak tomorrow morning. I'll let you get a couple of hours' sleep, then we'll figure out some way of getting you home. I probably won't be able to find Jordan, because by now he'll know I'm gunning for him. But he's got no car, that'll slow him down.'

Anguish was in Rowan's eyes. Jordan had her car.

Would she ever see it again? Would she ever see him again? And Regan! Regan would hardly want to meet a stranger who had ruined her plans. Why didn't Drew tell her what was so catastrophic about going to a local dance with Jordan? Okay, so she had worn a startling dress, and had danced like a whirling dervish, but the ordinary guests had not known she was drunk or drugged. Drew had saved her from that.

Suddenly Drew's mood changed and angrily he dropped her hand, demanding, fiercely, 'Why? I can't understand why you'd throw it all away on that young scoundrel . . . He's no good for you or any other decent girl. He's a conniving son of a gun, and you should know it more than most. You've grown up next door to him. Oh, you've always loved him, I know that, but you've been aware of what he is. You look at him and see something different from the rest of us mortals. You think there's something fine, something decent waiting to come out of his character. Well, there isn't. He's totally irresponsible, without conscience.'

He stood up, a tall powerful figure, broad-shouldered and athletically built, and paced the length of the small room several times trying to get his anger under control. Then he leaned down towards her. 'Have you thought what would be happening to you now if I had not come home? Do you know what his intentions were towards you tonight? Well, I do. He was openly boasting of it at the bar earlier tonight. Brent told me when I arrived.'

'No,' Rowan managed the one syllable negative like an explosion, her eyes wide with shock.

'Yes, oh, yes indeed. And what would you have done to disappoint him? You couldn't have fought him off. Look at you! I could do anything I wanted to you lying there, and you couldn't stop me or even call out for help. You disgust me.' He swung away and continued his pacing, his tanned face showing the tension he was under. 'And who could blame him? You tarted up like that, dancing like a wild thing, there wasn't a man in the room not touched by your exhibition. *Even me!* And I've known you and treated you like a kid sister since the day you could walk. I'm glad you've mucked up your only chance to leave home. You're not fit to be away from your father's protection. He should chain you to your bed, or get you fitted with a chastity belt!'

He went out slamming the door behind him.

Rowan was outraged by his words, yet not doubting for an instant that Jordan had planned to destroy Regan's reputation that night. Revulsion swept over her. She had so lightly thought she could correct any false impressions the following day. If Drew had not arrived she would have been completely at Jordan's mercy, and she would never have received any sympathy from the crowd at the dance, because her behaviour would have been seen to be flamboyant and tantalising. Dear God, what a fool she had been!

When Drew stepped back into the room her eyes flew to his face.

'You don't have to be afraid of me, Regan,' he said very quietly. He sat down and caught her hand in his. 'I apologise for that outburst. And it's not you I'm disgusted with, but myself. Forgive me, I shouldn't have frightened you like that. You're so damned innocent. Your father has kept you shut away from the world, not allowing you to mix with young people of your own age, never allowing you to go to parties or dances, or even a film. You've not got a television in your house and even now your reading is censored. I've told and told Daniel that in isolating you from the world he was making you more vulnerable.'

He sighed deeply and ran his hand through his thick dark hair. 'Ever since your mother died he's guarded your every step. It's criminal. You've been an exemplary daughter, you've never shown any rebellious streak, or any sign of running wild like the other teenagers—why couldn't he have trusted you more? But you've always clung to the idea that if you obeyed him in everything, one day he would trust you and let you follow the career of your heart. And you were right. You'd won, *dammit*, you'd won! By being virtually a slave on that farm, and being loyal, loving and obedient, you got his blessing to go overseas for that Art Scholarship for a year.'

Rowan stared back into his dark grey eyes with stunned incredulity. That's what she had done to Regan! She had blown her one chance of becoming independent. She closed her eyes, and turned her head aside so that he couldn't see the pain she felt. In her anguish of heart she mumbled, 'Jordan.'

'Yes, Jordan,' Drew answered heavily. 'Your father even agreed that if Jordan pulled up his socks and worked on the farm for a year and proved he could be a responsible adult, then . . .' He sighed deeply. 'That was Jordan's only hope. People can change. I honestly thought he loved you enough to make the effort. You are the only person who has ever had any faith in him, and I thought he'd do it for your sake. I've tried to reach him in every way I know how—to understand him, to help him—but his mother has planted such seeds of bitterness between us, there was just suspicion and hatred, nothing to build on.'

Rowan wished he would stop talking and go away. She just wanted to die. By her stupidity she had sabotaged Regan's chance of happiness in a really spectacular way. Why didn't he just leave her? That was easy . . . he thought she *was* Regan and he was trying to help.

'All in your hand, all you ever dreamed about, and because Jordan tricked you, you've lost the lot. Can you imagine your father's hurt in all this? Oh, sure, he'll be angry, but hurt also, and all the people who've loved and admired you so much. *Damn Jordan!* He would have it all worked out. He agreed to your going away, acted so delighted at having a chance to win your father's approval, and all the time he was planning this, either to get you pregnant so you'd have to marry him, or just to smash your father's trust in you so that he wouldn't let you go abroad. I can't believe that anyone who loved you would stoop to such low tactics . . . and he's my brother. Thank God Dad is dead and didn't live to see him grow up—he would have been ashamed of him. I hope his mother's satisfied with this night's work. She has spoiled him rotten all his life.'

Drew stood up and tucked the rug about her more snugly, then dropped a kiss on her cheek. 'Have a sleep, Regan. There's no use crying over spilt milk, we'll work on the mopping up job tomorrow. You can count on me, you know that, mate. I'll come back in a couple of hours and take you home. We'll face your father together—we'll think of something. I'd offer to marry you myself, just to set you free to utilise that fantastic talent of yours, but that wouldn't work. With your crazy principles you wouldn't consider a divorce, so you'd be stuck with me for life, and I'm no bargain. You wouldn't mess up my life because I have no intention of ever getting married, so a nominal marriage with a quick divorce wouldn't faze me. Anyway, think about it.

He walked out, leaving Rowan with nothing to do but think. She couldn't sleep, and she wished she could just self-destruct. She had never in her whole life betrayed a friend, or deliberately set out to hurt anyone, and it was unbearable to know that she had injured her sister beyond healing. She had been so excited at the news that she had a twin sister, so full of enthusiasm to search her out and make herself known, to love her, and now . . . That father sounded a straight-laced fanatic; if she went to him and explained her part in it, provided he would speak to her, she knew instinctively that he would just think Regan would behave like her if she was allowed to leave home. She had done the damage, and it seemed beyond repair.

She thought of Drew. What a fantastic friend Regan had in that man. Regan must be quite a girl to have won the love of Jordan, and the strong friendship of a man like Drew. Rowan was deeply grateful that he had rescued her from Jordan, and for his kindness, even if it wasn't meant for her. She shuddered to think of what he would say when he found out she wasn't Regan. Would he be sorry he had protected her, or think that she deserved all she had been heading for?

She twisted in the bed and face down wept bitter tears for the predicament she found herself in. She wanted her mother and father, but even they wouldn't have been able to help. They would commiserate with her, and comfort her, but never in their most vivid imaginings would they have expected her adventure to end in such a crushing defeat. She had only herself to blame. She had been brought up in Auckland, she wasn't a naïve, trusting, simple country girl, yet she had never met anyone as despicable as that Jordan.

Eventually Rowan stopped crying, but it was ages before she realised that if she could turn over on the bunk, she should have movement back in her legs. She wriggled her toes, then her feet, then her knees, then joyfully flung back the rug. She stood up and walked to the window, and her heart thrilled at the early morning beauty of the bay. Fishing boats were chugging their way down the channel in the pearly morning light, and she quickly put on her shoes and wrapped her shawl around her shoulders, hurrying out of the cabin.

It was heaven to be able to walk again—she had felt so helpless lying there. The street lights were still on, but the street was deserted, and she began to run. She wanted to get back to the house on the hill before anyone woke up and saw her in her dance dress. She took deep breaths of the crisp, fantastic sea air and her spirits rose. The house on the hill was her sanctuary. Drew had said he would come back, and she didn't want to meet him. She wanted to hide until she had herself sorted out. Breathlessly, she climbed the hill just as the sun was tinting the horizon and she flew in the back door and shut it behind her with a sense of overwhelming relief. The sudden spurt of energy was leaving and she felt her strength ebbing again, but she was safe, despite the dull throbbing in her head.

But was she? Jordan might be there. Shakily she forced herself to go to the garage, but it was empty. She took a deep breath, then carefully checked the other rooms—she was alone. Relieved, Rowan locked the doors and decided to have a shower. The force of streaming hot water made her feel clean, but not refreshed, so she slipped on her pyjamas and crawled into bed and fell asleep.

It was late in the afternoon when she woke, and as the recent events came back to her, she felt hollow and aching despair. Defeat, like a heavy weight, sat on her chest. The taste of failure was bitter in her mouth. Nothing in her life had prepared her for such a terrible time. She had been so happy, so excited about her search, so near to success, then *Jordan*.

Wearily she walked through to the kitchen and made herself a drink of coffee and a sandwich. Feeling a little better, she rang her parents and poured the whole rotten story into their loving, sympathetic ears.

Her mother's reaction was predictable. 'Come home immediately, darling. I wish we'd never made that promise. I can't bear to hear you so crushed. Come home . . .'

'You don't want to do that, do you, Rowan?' her father demanded sharply over the extension. 'You need to see this thing through.'

'Through to what?' Rowan asked sadly. 'Regan won't want even to talk to me. I've ruined her life, spoiled everything she's ever worked for. Her father won't let me near her, you can bet on that, and she obeys him in everything. What reason has she to want to meet me?'

'The same reason you have for wanting to meet her,' her father told her briskly. 'Curiosity. She won't be able to resist getting a look at you. Stop being so maudlin . . .'

'*Maudlin!*' Rowan shouted angrily, outraged at his change of tone. 'I don't even know what it means . . .'

'Weakly sentimental, tearful, drowned in self-pity. Start fighting back.'

'Fighting whom?' Rowan yelled. 'Jordan? Drew? Regan? The whole darned community?'

'Why not?' her father demanded bracingly. 'You're not a weakling, have some gumption.'

'Put some in the mail for me,' Rowan said sarcastically. 'You don't know what this place is like. It's a very beautiful place, but isolated, and everyone knows everyone else, and they have already made their minds up about me. No one would help me, they'll despise me for my behaviour last night. They'll protect Regan from me—she's a local girl, and well liked, too.'

'Then you'll have to work at changing their minds. Use your brains, Rowan. You've taken that house for a month, try and fit into the local scene. Don't move too fast, just watch for any opportunity. Be positive in your approach to people . . .'

'If Jordan was here I'd be positive all right,' Rowan said angrily.

Her father laughed, 'That's it, show a bit of spirit, Princess. You've got a terrific personality, a bright mind, and talent that you haven't even discovered. Find yourself down there, then sell yourself. Believe me, they'll be eating out of your hand by the end of the month. I've got confidence in you.'

'Huh! That makes one,' Rowan offered glumly.

'Do you want to come home beaten, your tail between

your legs like a dog that's cowed, your dreams in tatters?'

'No, I don't,' Rowan exploded.

'Well, that's the only other alternative. Keep in touch.' The phone went dead.

Angrily Rowan went back to her bedroom and flung herself into blue jeans and a bright red top, thrusting her feet into her sandals. Who could have imagined her father being so uncaring? Telling her to stand her ground and fight! He hadn't a clue of the situation she was in. She felt if she was going to fight with anyone she would pick on him for starters.

She brushed her hair and caught it back in a scarlet ribbon, and marched out of the house and down the hill. Who did this lot think they were to judge her on one night's performance? She'd show them . . . and that Drew, too. She suddenly laughed. Her father was one heck of a smart guy. Here she was, her fighting blood aroused, tramping down the village street like a warrior scenting battle, and only half an hour ago she had been wallowing in self-pity.

Rowan looked about her with renewed interest. It was such a pretty little town. She sat down on the steps of a monument below the church on the hill and gazed out across the Bay towards the bush-covered blue hills surrounding it, then down the main street where safari tourist buses were loading passengers; there was lots to do and to see around here. Not many local people were about at this time of day, but during the working week they would be in for shopping and mail, and she would get to know them. And one of them would be Regan.

Her spirits soared. Her father was right—Regan wouldn't be normal if she didn't want to get a look at her double. And in such a small community, there really wouldn't be any way to avoid her. She might even get a job—well, there was nothing to stop her from trying. She watched the big Land Rovers pull out, and saw Farewell

Spit Safari written on the side. She would love a trip out there.

Rowan saw some children playing on the big black traction engine displayed on a concrete block on a green in front of the local Fire Station. Then the doors of the station opened and out came a group of men in Fire Brigade uniforms and started their practice. Now *they* would have to be locals, Rowan thought, as a town this size would only have a volunteer Fire Brigade. What a handsome lot they looked in their attractive uniforms, fit and bronzed-looking. Oh, there would be oodles of opportunity for her to get information. Jordan and Drew Hewitt weren't the only pebbles on the beach.

Thinking about the beach, she decided to go for a run. Jauntily, she strolled down the street past the Lighthouse Lodge, and when she heard a wolf-whistle rend the air she didn't look round, though her smile broadened. Rowan knew it had been for her and it encouraged her. She had plenty of time . . . a whole month to make herself known, and she chuckled. She would have to work on her image— she would have to be very demure and circumspect to eradicate the impression she had made last night. She would be friendly with women and children, and keep an aloof and cool distance from men.

The tide was on the turn and she could see the water creeping in to cover the mud flats, and as she walked along past the protection works, she admired the attractive houses and wonderful exotic flower-gardens and shrubs. Seagulls and numerous other birds crowded the sands and flats, and she startled them as she started to run, feeling a sense of exhilaration building up in her. She wasn't beaten, not by a long chalk, she was just beginning to enjoy herself.

The sand was firm under her feet, the fresh salt air filled her lungs, and the wind caught at her hair playfully as she settled down to a steady pace. She loved the beauty and emptiness of the fabulous beach. On her return trip, she saw a group near the old wharf piles and slowed her pace to a walk. A woman with two children was gathering pipis. She would do for a start.

Before she could think of some way to approach them, the little boy saw her and ran towards her, his face alight with joyful anticipation, 'Regan, Regan!'

She caught him up in her arms and found herself being hugged and kissed with great enthusiasm. Laughing, she responded, then lowered him to the sand. He was a gorgeous little fellow, about three years old, with red-gold hair, large horned-rimmed glasses and a mischievous grin. 'Hello, what are you doing here?'

'Chase water, chase pipis for Tinker. Mum, Hannah!' He dragged her, unresisting, towards a red-haired girl, about twenty-five.

'Hullo, Regan, I've never seen you down here jogging before. I thought you got enough exercise on the farm.'

Rowan grinned, her smile was infectious and bright. 'That's because I'm not Regan. My name is Rowan Chapman, but I'm quite happy to cash in on the obvious affection your son has for Regan.'

'What!' The girl's eyes widened in surprise, and her voice squeaked, 'Of course you're Regan, even Hannah knows that.'

Hannah, a blonde of about eighteen months, was staggering towards her, chuckling with delight, and then shrieking with excitement as Rowan tossed her in the air. 'Hello, honey,' she kissed the cute little dimpled girl.

'No, I'm not Regan, but she's a friend of yours, I gather.'

'I think you're having me on.' The dark girl looked at her dubiously. 'You must be. But why, for heaven's sake? You'll have me believing I'm losing my marbles if you don't explain.'

'My name is Rowan. I arrived here last night. I found

out a month ago that I had a twin sister, an identical twin, and I traced her this far. I believe she is Regan, but I haven't met her yet. Do you believe me?'

'I suppose I have to, but I feel silly, it's as if I've always known you and you're pretending to be a stranger.' She laughed, 'Okay, my name is Rochelle, I'm a solo mother, and Regan is a friend. This is Aaron and Hannah; no husband.'

'Pleased to meet you, Rochelle. Could you tell me Regan's surname?'

'Regan McKinnon. Oh, golly, does she know about you?'

Rowan switched Hannah on to her other arm. 'No, not yet . . . well, it depends. Jordan Hewitt knows I'm looking for her. He may have told her by now.'

'You know Jordan?'

'Unfortunately,' Rowan said shortly.

Rochelle laughed. 'He's a real character, that lad. You sound as if you've had a bad experience with him, but don't feel alone, he manages to shake most people. But, in spite of his tricks, he's got something that makes people forgive him. You won't stay mad long with him.'

'Want to bet?' Rowan's blue eyes sparkled.

'It would be like taking candy from a kid,' Rochelle said with a charming laugh. 'You'll see, he'll get around you. But what I meant was, does Regan know . . . Look, this may have been a shock for you, but it's going to be worse for Regan. I've known her a while and she's never mentioned that she's adopted. Maybe it just hasn't come up, but she may not know.'

Hannah was struggling to get down and Rowan released her before straightening to stare with wide blue eyes at Rochelle, 'Oh, no. People these days always tell the kids they're adopted. Her parents wouldn't be so stupid. Oh, how ghastly if I've done something even worse.'

'Even worse than what?' Rochelle stared back curiously.

'You'd better have it all, because I need a friend. Jordan took me to a dance here last night pretending that I was Regan . . . look, I didn't know what a restricted life she led . . .'

Understanding swept over Rochelle's attractive face. 'Now I know what all the gossip was about at the store this morning. It was all a bit scrappy to me, but they were talking about this fantastic girl Jordan was with, and her dress, and the way she danced, and how mad Drew was . . . You're the one.'

Rowan nodded ruefully.

'But no one said it was Regan . . . well, they wouldn't to me, because they'd know I was her friend. I mean, I'd slaughter them if they were saying those things about . . .' She suddenly put her hand over her mouth. 'Sorry, I'm sorry—and my big mouth.'

Rowan shrugged her shoulders. 'Forget it. I made a real nut of myself, quite an exhibition. I don't ordinarily act like that, but Jordan put something in my drink, and I guess I must have made Salome look a slouch. I do want to get in touch with Regan, to apologise. I didn't mean to hurt her reputation, my own either, if it comes to that. It was Jordan's idea, and as far as I'm concerned he can clear up the misunderstanding.'

Rochelle rescued Hannah from a sudden death by drowning, before continuing the conversation. 'I wouldn't let Jordan clear up any problem as far as I was concerned. He would just delight to make it ten times worse—he's a walking disaster area.'

'Well, what will I do? Will you help me? Couldn't you explain for me? She trusts you, and I'd be so grateful . . .'

'I'd have to see her face to face. I mean, if she thinks she's McKinnon's daughter and I blurt it out on the phone that she's adopted, it could be awful for her. She's such a sweet kid, I'd hate to hurt her.'

'So would I,' Rowan said with feeling. 'But it seems I've done nothing else since I arrived. Could you go and see her now, before the gossip reaches her?'

'She won't hear much, her father sees to that. And I can't go there; no car, for one thing, and we're not that close. I can't visit her home, her father only lets approved folk go there. I usually meet her down the street. Actually, Aaron fell in love with her, and made a fuss of her, so we got talking. She comes to visit me if she gets a few spare minutes when she's down for the mail, but her father would kill her if he knew. I mean, a woman with two kids and no husband—he takes a very narrow view of life. Look, come home and have tea with me, and we'll talk about the best way to handle this.'

'You *are* kind,' Rowan said with a grateful smile. 'I really am at a loss how to go ahead. But you could be wrong, I don't go around announcing to all and sundry that I'm adopted. If it comes up, I say so, and I think of my parents as the only ones in my life. We might be seeing difficulties where none exist.'

Rochelle shook her head. 'I hope so. Let's go.' She gathered up her scattered possessions, picked up Hannah, and called Aaron who was chasing seagulls with zest. 'I live up the hill straight beyond the garage.'

'So do I,' Rowan said, charmed by the coincidence. 'We're neighbours.'

'Great, I could do with someone young and cheerful next door. I do hope I've worn these two out so that they sleep tonight. Sleep is the most precious thing in the whole world to me, I never get enough as these two don't sleep well.'

It was only then that Rowan noticed the deep purple shadows under her new friend's eyes. She had been so concerned with her own problems that she'd been completely selfish. 'Maybe I can take your kids off your hands occasionally while I'm here. Can you sleep in the afternoon?'

'Can a duck swim? I could sleep standing up if these kids would give me a chance. You can have my undying gratitude, if you really mean it. But do you like kids?'

'Love them,' Rowan said cheerfully, catching Aaron's small hand and helping him over the rocks. 'I'm a kindergarten teacher.'

'A goldmine, a goldmine! I've struck it rich!' Rochelle danced and twirled around with happy laughter.

Rowan caught her up with a thoughtful expression on her face. 'Are there many mothers like you about? Aren't there any playschool or kindergarten activities here?'

'No kindy, playschool twice a week, but that's only for Aaron. And yes, there're plenty of tired, exhausted, hungover mums like me. We get together and moan. That helps, but not very much.'

Rowan's thoughts flew from one idea to another. She could start a crèche if there were enough children. That would surely bring her into contact with a section of the population, and if the word got round that she was capable with children, it must surely enhance her tattered reputation. Her father said to start slow, so she didn't mention her idea to Rochelle, but he had also said to be positive and grasp every opportunity. Could it be this *easy*?

'There's Drew Hewitt,' Rochelle exclaimed just as they reached the garage. 'Flag him down. I don't know him well, he's a big shot round here, but he's very pleasant and a friend of Regan's. Ask him if she knows she's adopted. If she knows, I'll try and get her on the phone and explain the other bit.'

Rowan stepped out on the road and raised her arm. As Drew braked on the oppostite side of the road, she ran towards him, her face aglow with pleasure. Now she could thank him for helping her last night.

Ignoring her brilliant smile, he sat coldly impassive watching her crossing the road. When she reached him he said sarcastically, 'I was wondering when you'd turn up. I knew you'd be all right, your sort always are. I want to offer my apologies for interrupting your evening with Jordan last night. I'm sorry you were disappointed at being snatched away from my brother, but as you were well aware, I mistook you for Regan, and *she* does have a reputation to protect.'

Rowan felt her colour rise as she became aware of the withering contempt in his cold grey eyes. 'But Jordan . . .'

'Oh, Jordan's okay. Worried about your little playmate, are you? That's nice. You'll find him at the pub. Where else would he be on a Saturday night? But I'd better warn you, he doesn't look as pretty as he did last night. Still, he must have known there'd be some repercussions after playing such a dirty trick on everyone.'

Rowan went white with anger. 'I wasn't in on the dirty trick. I was a victim, the same as the rest of you.'

'Pull the other leg. Jordan's explained how you planned it all for a laugh. And he's driving your car, so that speaks for itself. We don't like people like you in the village, and I suggest you move on. You'd find it pretty dull, anyway.'

'I want to see Regan.'

'I doubt that you will,' he informed her coldly. 'She's a decent kid, not your kind at all.' He depressed the accelerator and drove off, leaving her shaking in the middle of the road.

She walked back to Rochelle, almost swamped by the surges of anger and rage that swept over her. How dared he make such superficial judgments about her!

Rochelle looked at her with concern. 'What did he say to upset you? Doesn't Regan know?'

Rowan spluttered with anger, 'He's a sanctimonious, supercilious, pompous prig!'

'Oh, no, he isn't,' Rochelle replied gently. 'He's a really decent guy. Everyone likes Drew Hewitt.'

'*Not everyone,*' Rowan said through gritted teeth.

'You must have misunderstood him. He's a perfect gentleman . . .'

'He is not,' Rowan stormed. 'I'd rather have Jordan any day. At least you know to watch out for him, but that hypocrite, smarmy and smooth, pretending to be friendly and kind. He's the worst sort of man, the very worst sort.'

'Is that the first time you've met him?' Rochelle asked in anxious tones.

'No, but I surely hope it's the last, the arrogant beast. Let's forget about him and think of something nice.'

CHAPTER FOUR

ROWAN was glad the hill was so steep that it left her breathless. She didn't want to talk, not about Drew Hewitt. Last night at the dance she had seen the charming, handsome side of him—suave, sophisticated, convivial—then later the caring, concerned side, strong and protective, and she had envied Regan his friendship. But this time she had discovered another facet of him, hard and unforgiving, arrogant and contemptuous, and it hurt unbearably.

Not even Greg at his worst had been able to sear her with such scorn. She might, if she stayed long enough, manage to change some people's opinion of her, but she would never change *his* mind. He had despised her, and he had believed Jordan's story that she was part of the whole set-up. He thought she had purposely decided to destroy Regan, his friend, and he loathed her.

She enjoyed the evening with Rochelle, but even after the children were in bed and they sat lazily watching the TV programme, his strong dark face kept coming between her and the screen. No man had ever made such an impact on her. No man had ever made her so angry. He had diminished her within her own image of herself; she felt small and ineffectual, and *outraged*. She tried to concentrate on what Rochelle was saying during the commercial break.

'I was offered a job at the hospital, being a trained nurse, as I told you. I'd just love to take it, I need the money, but there's the complication of the kids. It would do me good to get back into the profession, and it would be better for the children if I was with adult company part of the time, but with shift work, I can't see how I could manage to get anyone to mind them at such odd hours.'

Rowan sighed. Another opportunity presenting itself. She was completely free, she could fit in, but the problem weighing on her now was, should she?

'What are you thinking about, Rowan? You look awfully troubled. Can I help?'

'I've got to know if Regan knows she's adopted. Who can I ask? If she thinks she's the natural daughter of the McKinnons', when I break the news . . . It doesn't bear thinking about. I could leave now and not cause any more furore. You are really the only person who knows the truth. You will keep it to yourself?'

'Of course I will. You can trust me. But all those people at the dance, and Jordan, they'll keep talking.'

'About what? They don't know anything. The dance crowd will continue to think it was Regan, even if she denies it, and Jordan only knows I was uncannily like her, but he has nothing to go on. People do have doubles—the Queen has one, they had a stand-in for Montgomery during the war, I remember seeing a film on it. If I left now, tonight, no one would be any the wiser. It would just be a great mystery.'

'You'd do that, leave without meeting your sister?' Rochelle looked at her incredulously. 'I thought it was all-important to you. You've spent weeks looking for her.'

'Yes, I would,' Rowan said fiercely. 'I couldn't live with myself if I destroyed her belief in her parents. But I've got to know. I want to meet her, desperately I want that, but not if it costs her her peace of mind. If I didn't know I was adopted and someone bounced up and told me, then I couldn't take anything my parents said as gospel ever again. It would tear apart the whole fabric of my life. Who will I ask?'

Rochelle frowned. 'Now I see it. Oh, Rowan, what a mess. Well, try her father, ring him up. He's bound to have heard something about last night. He'll be really worried, waiting for you to blow the gaff. If you put it to him straight, he should be really grateful that you are prepared to go away without telling Regan the truth.'

'What if he won't talk to me?'

'He hasn't got much option as far as I can see, not if he wants to keep you quiet.' She brushed her hand through her short red hair. 'Then there's Drew. He'd know for sure . . .'

'I won't talk to him,' Rowan said fiercely. Again his face presented itself to her mind, tanned, and strongly handsome, his grey eyes coldly contemptuous, and she stood up shaking. 'I'm going to go home now, if you don't mind. I'll ring her father. It's only nine o'clock, and he shouldn't be in bed yet.'

'If that's what you feel is right.' Rochelle stood up and walked to the door with her. 'Are you sure you're okay? Wouldn't you rather try from here? I hate to let you go on your own.'

Rowan threw her a grateful glance. 'You've been so kind. If I stay, we'll work something out together to give you a spell from the children, but if I have to go, I'll keep the thought of you as my most pleasant memory of Collingwood.' Tears blurred her eyes and she ran quickly down the track to her own place.

She found the phone book and searched the names, then dialled the McKinnons' number. It rang and rang and rang. She dialled again, still no answer. If only she had her car, she could drive up there . . . no, she couldn't, she might meet Regan. Where was Jordan? Down at the local pub, enjoying an evening's revelry with his friends, while she skulked up here hiding. Blast Jordan Hewitt! Blast his brother, Drew, too. If he had given her time, she could have had all this settled this afternoon.

She tried the McKinnons' number every ten minutes, getting more and more angry. She couldn't settle, and wandered out to the verandah, gazing across the still, quiet water of the Bay. Last night she had been having fun, enjoying herself with the crowd. Her anger centred on the Hewitts, so that when suddenly her persistent efforts elicited an answer, she had trouble concentrating.

'May I help you?' a deep masculine voice asked pleasantly.

'Is that Mr McKinnon?' Rowan asked nervously.

'No. The McKinnons are away. This is Drew Hewitt speaking. I'm a neighbour, we're on the same line. I have heard you ringing many times and thought I'd tell you to save yourself the trouble—they'll be away for several days.'

Her anger exploded. 'Are they, indeed? Well, Drew Hewitt, you'll do nicely. This is Rowan Chapman speaking and you can tell your brother Jordan to bring my car back. If it's not here by nine o'clock tomorrow, I'm ringing the police. He took it without my permission, and I'm reporting it as stolen. Furthermore, you can come and see me yourself either tonight or by nine tomorrow, or my next move will have worse consequences for your little mate Regan, and not even your Sir Galahad protection will save her!'

Rowan banged down the receiver before he could answer. She walked through to the lounge and punched the TV knob, then flung herself on to the sofa. She hadn't meant to say any of those things, but she wasn't sorry. She needed her car, and if it meant going to the police, she would do just that. Who did these Hewitts think they were?

She chuckled as she tried to imagine Drew's face when she hung up. That would teach him to look at her with utter loathing. There was nothing more infuriating than to have a telephone banged down in your ear . . . yes, there was; the way he drove off leaving her humiliated in the middle of the road that afternoon.

As she snuggled down in bed, she knew she had been foolish to threaten him. It was an empty threat, because she knew she wouldn't do anything to upset Regan. But he didn't know that. Maybe he would turn up? He believed her capable of any infamy, so his own nasty mind would draw him into making some sort of response to her demand.

Next morning she sat sunning herself on the front verandah, watching a fantastic display of two men on water skis. It was a brilliant morning, the sun sparkling on the smiling blue water and the spray from the boat and the weaving figures curving clear and glorious behind them. She felt bold and confident, and dressed accordingly in bold colours. Her well-cut emerald slacks and yellow top emphasised and even exaggerated her good points. She liked bright colours, and she wanted all the advantage she could gain as she waited for the Hewitt brothers to appear. She had no doubt they would.

Her small attractive face lit with a smile of anticipation as she heard the throaty roar of her Mazda take the hill. So it was going to be Jordan first. She heard him reverse into the garage and the motor die, then his steps coming along the verandah, and her blue eyes gleamed.

Suddenly around the corner a cap came flying towards her. She caught it and put it on her head at a rakish angle and waited.

Jordan poked his head around the corner. 'It's always wise to throw your hat in first. If it gets a good reception, then it's safe to follow.' He stood, wearing only shorts, sandals and a gold chain which hung around his bronzed neck, arrogantly sure of the perfection of his well-muscled body.

'Not all that safe,' Rowan warned him.

He walked towards her, a mischievous smile on his good-looking face. 'You look dressed to kill . . . not me, I hope.' He eased himself down beside her.

Rowan broke into a delighted laugh. 'Somebody beat me to it. What a fantastic black eye, so colourful: blue, purple, red and black.'

'You're a sadist.' Jordan fingered his injured eye tenderly. 'Regan would have been all sympathy.'

'I'd love to black the other one,' Rowan told him firmly. 'Did you walk into a door?'

'No. I walked into Drew on Friday night, and he laid one on me. He didn't give me time to explain. He thought he was defending Regan's honour and he didn't half do a bad job. I reckon he loosened a couple of my teeth, too.'

'Great,' Rowan said with satisfaction. 'You deserved everything you got.' Then she stared at him with curiosity. 'You sound almost proud that Drew beat you up.'

He grinned with great charm. 'I am, in a way. He's never done that before. Made him almost human to do his block like any ordinary guy. You can have a bit too much of his long-suffering patient attempts to reason and reach an understanding.'

'I hope he hits you again, and often,' Rowan said flatly. 'Seems to have done you good.'

Jordan's greeny eyes lit with malicious amusement. 'Oh, it did me good all right. When he found out he'd made an ass of himself for the wrong girl, he had to apologise. That doesn't happen often in our family—I'm the one usually in the wrong. I tell you, it took all the pain away. I was going to wear a black patch, even tried one on, and I looked devilishly handsome in it too, but there was too much joy in leaving it naked and watching him feel guilty.'

'You're detestable. He has no need to feel guilty, and I'm only grateful that he whisked me out of the Hall. He acted like a gentleman.'

'You wouldn't say that if you heard his description of you when he found we'd tricked him. He was sparking on all cylinders.'

'*We* tricked him,' Rowan shouted indignantly. 'You're a liar! It was all your idea.'

'How could he know that?' Jordan's face was all innocence. 'And what did he say to you, while he thought you were Regan? A simple mistake couldn't bring him to the boil. He doesn't rile easily, my big brother. He must have said something incriminating, think back. It could be useful for us.'

'For us?' Rowan gave him a scathing glance. 'I'll never be caught by you again, Jordan.'

Jordan laughed, his white teeth flashing against his deep tan. 'I wouldn't be too sure. I'm very devious. And I'm the only one who can help you get alongside Regan. You'd better be nice to me.'

'I'd rather trust a rattlesnake,' Rowan said crushingly.

'Now honestly, what harm have I done you? I brought you over the mountains to the very valley Regan lives in. You wouldn't have found her except for me. I took you to dinner and you enjoyed yourself, and I danced with you and you were having a ball until Drew spoiled it. I promise you, you would have enjoyed the rest of it, too . . .'

'Get out!' Rowan said furiously, getting to her feet. 'Out! I never want to see you again.'

Jordan scrambled to his feet and avoided her easily, laughing wickedly. 'I'll go now, but I'll be back, and you'll be delighted to see me. I've brought your car back. I've got you a place to live in. What are you so mad about? You're a super-looking wench, and I'll be happy to take you out any time you ask me . . .'

Glaring, she watched him drop over the wall and heard him whistling his way down the hill. She had let him off too easily, but as the sound died away she found herself smiling. He was smart, the way he had focussed her attention on the things he had accomplished for her, and avoiding the monstrous motives behind his actions, then provoking her to rage so that he had an excuse to leave. No wonder Regan loved him. Any girl would be attracted to the incredible sensual power of his magnificent physique, and his undoubted charm. He *was* hard to resist, an exciting personality, a rebel, quite unprincipled, yet not a mindless fool, and there was exceptional intelligence in those smiling hazel eyes.

He was right—when he came back she would be delighted to see him. Was his appeal the fact that he presented such a challenge? Poor Regan if she hoped to change him into a conforming individual! A hopeless project.

'I see Jordan has been—you have your car parked safely in the garage. What did you want to see me for?'

Rowan stiffened in surprise, before turning to face Jordan's stern brother. Her blue eyes narrowed dangerously as she took in the complete contrast he presented compared to Jordan. Immaculately attired in well-cut grey slacks, and tailored sports jacket, shirt and tie perfectly matched and highly polished shoes, he was the epitome of the wealthy country gentleman.

'Thank you for coming,' she said with remarkable lack of emotion, but her blue eyes challenged the hardness of his grey gaze. 'If you had been a little more polite yesterday, this meeting would not have been necessary.'

'It's no pleasure for me to be here, and your threats don't frighten me. I think your actions have totally discredited you from any normal consideration, good manners included. I am only here to see if I can dissuade you from hurting a dear friend of mine. What is it you're after? Money?' His eyes glinted scornfully.

Rowan flung her head back, taunting him. 'How much are you prepared to offer?'

'So that's what it's all about,' he said in disgust. 'With your looks and talent I'm sure you'd find an easier way to separate men from their money than by trying to threaten me, or blackmail poor old Daniel McKinnon.'

His meaning was unmistakable, and Rowan felt her colour rising. She laughed in his face. 'How typical of your male chauvinist mind to think that selling my body would be the easier way.'

He stiffened angrily. 'I assure you, in this instance, I'm giving you sound advice. I have money, but not to give you, and McKinnon is a poor man unlikely to have the wherewithal to support you in the manner to which you would wish to become accustomed.'

Rowan's eyes were very blue as she smiled impudently at him. 'I am enchanted that you think I have the right qualifications for the work you suggest. Do you find me desirable? I'd value your opinion?' Very deliberately she started to weave in front of him, singing in a low, sexy voice a song she had done in an amateur theatrical revue.

'If you want my body,
And you think I'm sexy . . .'

'Behave yourself,' he said fiercely.

Rowan smiled wickedly. For a moment she had seen flare in his eyes something he probably wasn't even aware of. Jordan had been right. Drew had said something the other night that incriminated him. He had said, '*Even me.*' That was why he was so furious, because he had been stirred by her dancing as all the other men had in the Hall. As Jordan had confessed, it was nice to find Drew was human.

Dropping her pose, she said in her normal voice, 'Yes, I'll behave myself, if you will. I *am* insulted by your insinuations, but I will ignore them because I truly believe you are a friend of Regan's, and as such will give me the information I require. Contrary to your belief, I came here hoping to give her pleasure and great happiness. I am prepared to leave here within the hour if you will give me the answer to one question.'

'And that question is?' he asked warily.

She looked at him, trying to think how to frame her question. He was like Jordan in some ways, though not physically. He was taller, lean and hard, and she guessed tougher, but his personality was no less dynamic. He hadn't been behind the door when the good looks and charm were handed out in that family, but he was more dangerous than Jordan, enigmatic and controlled.

'Well?' he prompted her sharply, becoming restless under her scrutiny.

'Do you know that Regan is an adopted child of the McKinnons?' Rowan watched him carefully.

'No. Have you proof?'

'I can get it,' she informed him with assurance. 'I believe Regan and I are identical twins, that we were adopted into different families. I came here to find her.'

'That's ridiculous.' His tone was harsh but she could see doubt forming in his eyes.

'You can't tell there's any difference between us,' she challenged. 'If she was standing here beside me, could you say which one was which?'

'Probably,' he said carefully. 'Physically you're the same, but you are very different from Regan.'

'In that way?'

'I won't go into that.'

She laughed. 'Perhaps that is wise. I'm sorry that you don't know the answer to my question, so I can't leave. I will have to wait here until her father returns. Were her parents living here when she was born? Have you known her all her life?'

Drew seemed badly shaken. 'I suppose there could be some truth in what you're saying. The McKinnons came here when she was only a baby. They bought the farm next door. I never questioned that she was anything but their child, and I think she would have told me if she had known.'

Watching him, Rowan saw most of the anger drain away from him, and casually settled herself on the step. Not that she forgave him for his attitude, but there was no need to antagonise him further.

Hardly aware of what he was doing, he took a seat at the other end of the steps, his gaze going out across the Bay, as if it helped his concentration.

Turning sharply towards her, he demanded, 'You know what this will do to her if she finds out without any preparation?'

'I know.' Rowan met his gaze steadily.

He turned back to the view of the Bay, his mind obviously wrestling with the news it had received and trying to find an acceptable solution.

Rowan gave him all the time he needed.

At last he sighed, 'What do you propose to do?'

Rowan echoed his sigh, only just realising how intensely she had been waiting for his reaction. 'I'll stay here, out of sight, until they return . . .'

'It would be better if you went away. You could go to Nelson. I would get in touch with you after speaking to Daniel.'

'I wouldn't trust you to do that,' Rowan said sharply. 'I have had one experience with your family, and I don't want a repeat performance.'

'You think I'm like Jordan?' he glared at her, obviously incensed.

'No,' she answered calmly. 'I think Jordan is more predictable. He's an out and out rascal, but he doesn't pretend to be otherwise. I don't know about you. One moment you're friendly, the next scathingly sarcastic, treating me like a scarlet woman. How do I know you won't decide "out of sight, out of mind"? Problem settled.'

He had obvious trouble controlling his temper. 'I don't trust you either.'

Rowan smiled sweetly, 'Fine, we're agreed. What do

you suggest I do? Taking into account that I'm not leaving.'

He shrugged his shoulders. 'I suppose you could stay here. They'll be back Wednesday.'

'And you think I should remain a virtual prisoner in this house for the next three or four days? I can't see any harm in taking a look around the district. Jordan offered to take me sight-seeing.'

'You're not going with Jordan,' he exploded.

'Why not?' she demanded.

'You two have done enough already to damage Regan's reputation.' He stood up abruptly. 'If you want to see around the place, I'll take you myself.'

'You will?' Her eyes widened in astonishment.

'I will. If you're seen about with me, folk will just assume you're Regan; if you're with Jordan, they'll know you're not the authentic article.'

She chuckled at his description.

Impatiently he looked at his watch. 'I am going to church now. I'll come back for you at twelve. We'll go to Bonnie Doon and grab a picnic lunch, then you can say where you'd like to go.'

'Oh, I'll put myself completely in your hands,' she said with a wicked smile, knowing he was only taking her to protect Regan.

'I want your word that you won't go out with Jordan until we sort this out with Daniel.'

She saw the muscle in his cheek flick and knew how much it cost him to ask her. She was sorely tempted to tease him, but decided against it. 'Where's Bonnie Doon?'

'Where I farm up the valley.' There was unmistakable pride in his voice.

'I don't particularly want to meet Jordan's mother,' she protested.

'You won't. She's away at present. Jordan is going fishing so there will be no complications.'

'You mean we'll be *alone*?' Rowan couldn't resist lowering her voice, her big blue eyes wide and innocent.

He drew in his breath sharply. 'I'll be back at twelve.'

She chuckled as she watched him stride for the front gate, resentment evident in every brisk step. He hated to be responsible for her movements. The situation had improved as far as she was concerned. Instead of being pushed around, she was now doing a little of the shoving. The fact that it annoyed him immensely added an extra fillip of enjoyment to her day.

On the dot of twelve he tooted the horn at the gate and she grabbed a warm jacket and ran to join him in the station-wagon. Memories of the last time she was in it prodded her mind, and she fought to ignore them as he accelerated down the road and increased speed on the tarseal. She mustn't look back. Her father said to be positive, make every opportunity count.

They passed the wharf with two small fishing boats tied up, and above her she saw attractive motels on the brow of the hill. Straight on past the hospital and from there on, her only recollection afterwards was of an incredibly narrow country road, Drew's excessive speed, beautiful trees, huge mountains encircling the valley, farms and homesteads, some small, some large. She should have spoken when she got in, but she couldn't think of anything appropriate. Now the silence lengthened until it became burdensome.

She glanced at him, wondering what he was thinking. He must be regretting his offer. Drew's profile seemed carved out of granite, firm and hard set, but still the broad forehead, straight nose and well-shaped lips were very attractive. She wouldn't speak first, it was his party.

He flicked a glance at her. 'Nearly there.'

She smiled. 'Did you enjoy the church service?'

'Yes . . . pity you couldn't have gone. St Cuthbert's had its Centenary in 1973; it was quite an occasion. It's small, but beautifully situated overlooking the bay, and has an incredible sense of peace, for me at least. I'll get the gate.'

She looked up in surprise. There was no farm here, just a patch of native bush. She sat quietly while Drew drove through, then watched as he closed the gate. He followed a smooth dirt road through the bush, then changed down and forded a lively mountain stream. 'The Bonnie Doon stream,' he said laconically.

She gasped in delight as he drove on to the road again which curved around the bush to confront her with a fantastic green-grassed open valley where sheep and cattle grazed in an amphitheatre cradled in bush-clad hills. 'This is yours?'

'And Jordan's and my stepmother's.' His laughter contained no mirth. 'We don't pretend to play happy families here. I'd better warn you of that from the start.'

'Jordan has already done that,' Rowan said quietly, as she noted the neat tight lines of fences and sleek well-bred cattle. If Drew was responsible for all this, he had good reason to be proud. No wonder there was a feeling of bitterness in him because Jordan and his mother only took from this place and contributed nothing.

'If you believe everything Jordan tells you, you're less intelligent than you look.'

'You believed him when he said I deliberately set out to fool the people at the dance to hurt Regan,' she accused.

He didn't answer her, but swung round in a semi-circle in front of a large modern farmhouse. 'Come on in. I want to change, then we'll pack some food.'

She followed him into a large, elegantly furnished lounge, and looked about her with interest. There was luxury here, but it had a sterility, as if everything was set out in a showroom. Only some paintings on the wall gave it any personality. She wandered over to examine one, then recognised the scene as the almost secret entrance to this block of land. The artist had shown extraordinary talent, catching the privacy, capturing the brown-gold water of the Bonnie Doon stream, the huge native trees, and each delicate detail of the ferns and mosses. It drew her step by step into the centre until she lost all consciousness of being in a house, and could almost smell the dark earthy green scent of the bush, and feel the warmth of the sun where it streamed down through a break in the canopy of tree-tops.

'Impressed?' Drew asked.

'Oh, yes . . . impressed doesn't quite cover what I feel.' She turned, her eyes shining with appreciation. 'It has an extraordinary quality about it. I felt I was actually standing there, and the incredible silence . . .' She laughed a little breathlessly. 'I sound stupid, nobody can paint a silence.'

'Regan can, that's one of hers.' There was a satisfaction in his voice, almost a possessiveness.

'Regan painted that!' Rowan bit her lip, and felt the tears burn at her eyes. Her sister had this fantastic talent. 'What is she really like? I long to meet her.'

Drew looked at her flushed face. 'Regan is a very special girl . . . soft and gentle, and very loving. She has a transparent honesty, no covering mask, and what you see is what you get. She puts up no barriers, and consequently can be deeply hurt. That's why I try to protect her, especially from Jordan. So does her father. I don't say she lacks judgment, but that she sees people differently, in greater depth, with more perception, yet is completely without criticism. I'll get some bread and fillings for lunch.'

She saw him walk through to the kitchen through a blur of tears. He loved Regan; there was no doubt about that. 'Is there any more of her work here?'

'That one on the opposite wall. It's the moon rising out of the sea at Pakawau—well, before it rose. You see the orange glow over the water and the lighthouse beam from the Spit, and the softer lights to the north are the Japanese fishing fleet. It's a tremendous work, and out here are her sketches of Jordan and me. She likes landscapes and people best.'

Rowan studied the seascape, and found again the same quality of peace and utter silence and beauty. She looked across at the other painting and back. It was the light; the sun in one, the moon and lighthouse in the other, that gave a sense of power and great strength to them both. She walked through to where Drew, now changed into more casual clothes, was busy putting things into a cane hamper. 'Can I help?'

'It's no trouble,' he said off-handedly, as if he didn't want her close to him.

She went to the two sketches side by side on a cream wall. Just lines, bold heavy strokes . . . no, that wasn't true, the mouth and eyes held the key. Drew leaning forward smiling; Jordan serious and stern—just the opposite of the way she would have painted them. Jordan was always laughing, yet Regan knew these men as she did not. What had Regan seen that she did not? It was almost like talking with her sister, asking her opinion. And as she looked, it seemed to her that Jordan was tightly bound by heavy chains, in a strait-jacket, and Drew clear-eyed and free, at ease with himself.

Rowan closed her eyes. She must be seeing things of her own imagining. Those weren't their characters at all. Jordan was the free spirit, the carefree soul, and Drew the closed book, the conventional man bound by restrictions he put on himself. She looked again and it was there—both hard strong faces, yet there was openness in Drew's grey eyes and fear behind the green-hazel eyes. She was being fanciful. The sketches were black and white, no colour at all, how could she see green and grey?

'You said Regan was a neighbour. Where is her home?'

Drew turned. 'Go out the back door, that way.' His

bronzed hand pointed. 'They have a dairy farm, not a very good one. As I told you, Daniel hasn't much money.'

Rowan walked out through the door and across the yard. Beyond the well-painted sheds and barns which obviously belonged to Bonnie Doon, she saw a boundary fence and a small shabby house with an untidy yard and neglected-looking buildings. She went to lean on a five-bar gate and stared in dismay. The contrast of the two farms was startling: one superbly maintained with rich pastureland and good fences and gates and stock; the other forlorn and derelict, unpainted buildings and marshy ground with rushes and weeds rampant, fences and posts sagging. One spoke of wealth and the other of poverty.

She leaned her head against the wooden bars of the gate and burst into tears. That sad little house was where her sister lived, and she, Rowan, had been brought up in comparative luxury.

'Don't cry for Regan, she wouldn't thank you for pitying her. She has more happiness in that wee house than we have in our mansion, and probably than you have in yours.' Drew's voice was harsh and accusing. 'Regan has different values from most people. She's not materialistic, she has no envy in her make-up, no jealousy. She is the happiest person I know. It just wells up in her and overflows on to anyone who is around.'

Rowan tried to stop crying, but she felt crushed and bruised and empty. She had not ever imagined Regan being brought up any differently from herself. Of course, she knew that Regan's life had been restricted and isolated, but that house . . .

'I said Regan was soft and gentle, but I didn't say she was weak or sloppily sentimental. Stop crying. You're imagining yourself in her place, but you're not her. She grew up here, she loves this place, and she loves her father. Sure she wants to get away, but only to learn more about her painting and then she'll come back. She wouldn't be happy anywhere else. You're over-emotional, you're over-reacting.'

'Shut up! Leave me alone. Go away!' Rowan couldn't stop the flood of tears, and now her emotions were all twisted. Drew was condemning her for being what she was. He admired Regan and seemed to be saying that, compared to Regan, she was empty-headed and frivolous, concerned only with comfort and luxury. Perhaps she was, but she didn't need him to tell her so. She hated him. Would Regan think the same as Drew? They seemed very close. She *wanted* Regan to love her, and she wasn't worthless and materialistic, and she wasn't jealous or envious.

Drew touched her shoulder awkwardly. 'Don't cry, Rowan.'

That was the first time he had used her name, and the tears flowed faster.

Gently his hand stroked up and down her back, and she remembered the night he had danced with her, and his strong, supple hand soothing and supporting her. It was having the same effect now. Gradually the sobs slackened and she turned towards him to thank him, looking up at him with tear-drenched blue eyes and trembling lips.

Instantly his arms went round her, pulling her slender form against his taut strong body. His lips came down on hers with infinite tenderness and compassion, and she felt herself drowning in the sweetness of the experience. It was a sense of being in the centre of light—warm, soothed, comforted and happy. With pulses racing she moved closer into his embrace, feeling his hard lips on hers, and her arms went round his neck, holding him closer, longing for this sensation to go on forever.

When he raised his head, it was not compassion she saw in his eyes, but a longing that matched her own. It lasted only seconds then he forcefully put her from him, and strode angrily towards the station-wagon.

She followed him with a bemused smile on her face. She knew he was angry at himself and not at her. He had given part of himself away by showing his desire for her. Something in her stirred some emotion deep in him and he resented it. He didn't need to worry, she had no intention of binding him with unbreakable cords of love. She knew he had no intention of marrying. Well, she had none either. Greg had cured her of trusting her own judgment on men. But Greg's kisses had never had such a remarkable effect on her.

As he held the door of the car open for her, she smiled at him, taunting him with her blue eyes, letting him know that he had betrayed himself. She couldn't resist saying demurely, 'Thank you for being so kind.'

'*Kind!*' The word echoed explosively in the warm summer air and he slammed the door shut, then marched around the car and slid into his place and drove off without another word.

He was mad clear through. She wound down the window and felt the wind cool her face and blow through her hair. Once out on the road she said softly, 'It *was* kind. I suppose you have often comforted Regan that way if she was feeling miserable.'

'I have *never* comforted Regan that way,' he said furiously. 'What are you trying to prove? Regan is as different from you as chalk from cheese.'

She laughed outright. Joy like a river flowed over her at his answer. He *never* kissed Regan like that. Oh, she hoped he never would. She didn't want any other girl to share that fantastic sensation. She had envied Regan the pleasure of his friendship, the high opinion in which Drew held her, but she, Rowan, had something much better. He was fiercely resisting the physical attraction he felt for her, and she would use these three days to taunt him with it. That

should teach him to drive off and leave her humiliated in
the middle of the road. To heck with his good opinion. In
fact, the more he despised her, the more he would despise
himself for being drawn to her.

'Chalk and cheese, huh!' Amusement shone in her eyes
as he glanced at her. 'I suppose we are. After all I make my
money at this sort of thing. I'm not used to giving away
free samples.'

'That *you two* could be sisters!' he flung at her sarcastically, leaving the sordid comparison to her imagination.

'Where are we going for our picnic?' she demanded, the
lilt of laughter still evident in her voice.

He pointed to a signpost on the corner. 'I should take
you up there to the Devil's Boots. You'd feel right at
home.'

She chuckled. 'What are they?'

'A pair of boots, a natural rock formation, but I'll let
Jordan take you there. It should suit the pair of you, you
have a lot in common.'

'My goodness, it's fortunate that you're different from
Regan. You said she is uncritical of people, and *you* judge
them on a sliding scale, all downhill. You shouldn't be so
hasty in condemning me. After all, I've given up three
days of good business prospects to wait around for the
McKinnons to come home. I saw the volunteer firemen at
practice last night, a handsome lot they were. I should
turn a fair profit there. One of them whistled after me as I
walked down the beach.'

'You'd be disappointed, most of them are married,' he
said contemptuously.

She laughed again, 'And when has marriage interfered
with a man's appreciation of the finer things in life?'

Drew swung the car off the road on to the green verge,
and slammed on the brakes. 'You just quit your play-
acting. Okay, I deserve it. I should have apologised
before, about my behaviour on Saturday afternoon. It

was unforgivable. Will you accept my sincere apologies?'

His smile had immense charm and, in spite of herself, she felt the hardness that had formed around her heart melting like ice in the sun. It just disappeared, leaving her soft and completely vulnerable. 'I accept it,' she said a trifle breathlessly.

'What is your profession?'

'I'm a kindergarten teacher, but there are no vacancies at present.'

'That's where I see you, among small children. I bet they love you.' He turned on the engine and soon they were speeding back towards Collingwood.

Rowan sat stunned and silent. She felt all the tension ease away from him, and she loved his remark about the children liking her. But she had been using her hurt and anger as a shield against him, even a sword to whack him with, and it was gone. In its place was the terrifying thought that she might find his friendship more than she could handle.

She thought of the sketch Regan had made of him, the way she had caught the kindness, the humour, and the strength of Drew, in his eyes. He had said Regan didn't put up barriers; to look was to see. Well, he wouldn't find her so simple. She would put up a screen between them, she would use Regan, or Jordan, to hide behind so that he would never know what she was beginning to suspect was the truth: that as he was drawn to her, so she was also drawn towards him.

'We're not going far. Just to the Pupu Springs. There're plenty of fantastic spots in Collingwood itself, but by heading this way we are not so liable to run into people who would know Regan. We can't go too far because I have to milk Daniel's cows while he's away.'

'*You* milk cows!' she asked incredulously looking at his casual elegance.

He turned and winked at her. 'You've got a lot to learn about me, Rowan. I'm very versatile. And I'm guessing I have a lot to learn about you. It's such a strange feeling looking at you, the image of Regan who I know so well, and discovering you, a complete stranger. I find it intriguing, don't you?'

'So does Jordan,' she said lightly, feeling her heart start to pound.

'Yes, he would.' His voice was grim and his smile was gone.

'He says Regan and I are like lemon meringue pie, sweet and sour pickles. I gather I'm the sharp and bitter one, but he enjoys it.' She said it deliberately, knowing it would annoy him, and enjoyed seeing that give-away muscle flick on his tanned cheek.

'We turn down here this side of the Waitapu River. It's a narrow gravel road into the Springs, about two or three kilometres. We'll have lunch by the small wooden bridge near the Springs and walk in afterwards.'

'You're the boss,' she said agreeably. 'Can I watch you milk the cows? I've never been on a dairy farm.'

'Sure. As I said, it's not a good unit. We have many excellent and progressive farms in the district. I'll take you to some friends of mine when the McKinnons are back, and you'll see a really modern place, two hundred cows an hour and many of the routine functions programmed into a computer to save labour.'

'Why is the McKinnons' place so backward?'

'Oh, that's just Daniel. He's a Scot, and has all the stubborn independence that goes with that lot. He's a fine man and a good neighbour, but won't borrow money to do up his place. He wants to improve the property from income, and that's a long, slow haul. Then they've had a lot of bad luck. Funny how some people seem to have a tougher row to hoe than the rest of us. Losing his wife four years ago almost finished him. He lost interest in the place—just maintained it, that's all. And he bought hungry country, against my father's advice years ago.'

They had their meal in a clearing by a crystal-clear stream amid the native trees and the sun streamed down from a cloudless sky. Rowan was really hungry and enjoyed the meal, but her mind was never still. She would be on Regan's farm tonight. The second look at it would not hit her so hard. Off on a tangent, her thoughts flew to her parents and her next talk with them. Then, as her eyes lingered on Drew's face, she grew nervous. His complete acceptance of her awed her. She would rather that he kept a safe distance from her, conversationally as well as physically.

She walked along the glade path through the ferns and trees and was enchanted with the Dancing Sands Springs, which welled up in pure, clear, shallow water only two feet deep. One large spring, then hundreds of tiny ones stirring the sands, beautiful beyond description.

'Come on along to the Main Spring where there's a spectators' stand. It's fascinating to watch that tremendous flow of water thrust up from the green depths below at the rate of more than three thousand gallons per second.'

She followed him eagerly, a look of happy anticipation on her vivacious face, up the steps of the solid platform perched on the edge of the still pond and stared down where the waters welled up, endlessly. All around the throat of the Spring water, weeds floated and trembled among the intense blue-green, crystal-clear, pure waters, and the river rippled away to the north across open farmland. But Rowan's eyes were drawn back helplessly to the water boiling smoothly cold out of the depths of the earth, welling and welling, without end, hypnotic in its power.

'Well, what do you think of it?'

'Beautiful, incredibly beautiful. I could stand here all

day. There's a mystique, a spiritual quality that speaks of a power beyond ourselves, like God's love pouring out on the earth. It's like that bit that says boundless love that never ceases, cannot be stopped, that we may never know the height, nor depth, nor width of it, and will never come to the end of it. And it's quiet, no noise. I find it cleansing and soothing . . . awesome.'

'It has that effect on me, too, and many others. All sorts of myths and legends have been passed down about the mysterious source of this water, travelling perhaps from the centre of the Southern Alps, seeping down through mountains and valleys, taking perhaps a year or longer to reach this point. It's affected by earth tides, not sea tides, and has been measured at two hundred and sixty-six million gallons per day.'

'It's amazing.' Rowan was back to watching the glorious flow. Yes, it was love that came to her mind, that love her father spoke of: true loving, which stirs the spirit and soul; that rapture, that delight which binds with unbreakable cords the hearts of those who love each other.

She felt Drew's arm on her shoulder casually moving her to view another aspect of the phenomenon, but at his touch she trembled as some inner knowledge warned her that if she wasn't careful, a force as great as this water could flow between them, powerful and unstoppable and unending—and she wasn't ready for that.

He said quietly, 'I've seen divers in all their gear going down into that centre and being thrust back to the surface by the sheer force of it. It's amazing to think that Christchurch City uses about thirty-five million gallons of water a day to supply the needs of the population, so therefore this one spring could supply a city of two million people.'

Slowly she turned to look into his eyes, desperately needing to know whether he was aware of the danger that threatened to sweep away all her preconceived notions and his, and once started would be as unstoppable as the

Springs. His piercing grey eyes caught and held hers and she had her answer. He was more aware than her of what was happening, and even more determined than her that it would have no beginning.

Relieved, she said quickly, 'Shouldn't we be getting back to milk those cows?'

'You're right, we should be moving.' But he continued to stand there, his hand warm on her bare shoulder, staring down at the water for long silent minutes.

As they came down the steps and paused for another look at the Dancing Springs, she felt a great sense of sadness and loss as if she had side-stepped the most wonderful experience life could offer.

CHAPTER FIVE

As they drove back towards Bonnie Doon Rowan took a new interest in the dairy farms they passed, asking Drew the names of the people who lived there and noticing how attractive and modern the homes and sheds appeared, observing, too, the good pastures and well-fenced properties. And again her heart hurt for Regan as she tried to prepare herself for another sight of the McKinnon farm. This Golden Bay land was highly productive and very prosperous, so why did the McKinnons' place not have the same cared-for appearance?

'Come along, I want to introduce you to a friend of mine.' Drew came to join her where she sat in the brilliant late afternoon sunshine.

She looked up in surprise. 'I thought there was no one here.'

He grinned happily as he thrust his feet into his gumboots. 'This is going to be funny, watching Khan's reaction.'

Wondering, she followed him and stopped in amazement as he loosed a fabulous Alsatian which leapt on him, barking with excitement, then turned and flung himself against her in wild exuberance, licking her face and nearly overbalancing her, then dropping to the ground with a bewildered look on his intelligent face.

'Don't be scared,' Drew assured her. 'He's perfectly behaved towards my friends and he loves Regan. Just stand quietly until he sorts out his problem. You've thrown him, as you have me.'

Khan came forward slowly, his ears pricked and his tail waving slowly from side to side, his golden eyes full of questions. Then, apparently deciding it was all beyond him, he leaned against her with affection and she bent to stroke him. 'He's gorgeous.'

'He is,' Drew agreed. 'Throw him a stick—Regan always plays his silly games. He's not outgrown his puppy ways even though he's grown to such massive proportions. I was hoping he'd take to you, because I don't like the thought of you in that big house on your own. I'll give you Khan for protection while you're here. You'll find he's a good watch-dog, and is pretty frightening when he goes into his act. No one will trouble you, that's a promise.'

'Even Jordan?'

'Especially Jordan,' he said with great satisfaction.

She giggled—Jordan wasn't the only devious one in the family. Drew was quite able to protect what he considered his property. At that thought, Rowan's smile faded—she certainly wasn't that.

Wearing a pair of gumboots belonging to Regan which Drew fetched for her, Rowan found herself really enjoying the next two hours in his company. Walking down the lane behind the herd of huge Friesian cows, after sitting high on the yard rails watching Drew competently and efficiently move through the sequence of work which transferred the huge volume of milk from the cows to the gleaming milk tank, Rowan was impressed.

'Why is his milking shed and equipment so new and sparkling compared with everything else around here?' she demanded.

'Has to be. That's his livelihood. The laws and regulations governing milk production are very strict, and he wouldn't last five minutes in the business if the dairy inspectors found anything out of place. You wouldn't know, but these cows are high-producing pedigrees. He knows how to look after animals and he has some good land. The worst of it is about the house.'

'But the fences . . . compared to yours,' she protested.

He laughed, 'You're forgetting two things—these are electrified so he only needs a couple of wires, and dairy cows are quiet, contented animals. It's not like trying to keep track of sheep and beef cattle.'

After he had showered and changed, Rowan helped him prepare and share a pleasant meal. He was charming, friendly and entertaining, and Rowan had to force herself to think back how far they had moved since his angry arrival that morning. Considering the gamut of emotions she had survived from Jordan's appearance until now, it seemed more than a day in time, more like a year, yet here she was clearing the dishes, relaxed and laughing with him as if she had known him all her life.

As he moved to put on the stereo and dreamy music flooded the room she walked swiftly to the two portraits on the wall. Events were moving too fast for her. She wanted to apply the brakes, to move cautiously forward. What had Regan felt for these two paintings she had drawn so skilfully? They were both so different from any men she had ever come in contact with, forceful and exciting personalities, good-looking and self-confident—overpowering was the word she was searching for. They were both using her for their own ends, she was sure of that, but wasn't she doing just the same? Using them to get close to Regan? But they were stronger, tougher than she was, and she knew that she had only the faintest inkling of the stresses and strains which forced these men into some bitter competitive conflict. She didn't want to get hurt in it all but, even as she tried to withdraw, she knew that she found it exhilarating to be involved.

Drew stood beside her, a curious, unreadable expression in his eyes. 'Have you enjoyed the day?'

'Yes, very much. I've loved it.' Why was she trembling?

'Then I'll claim a reward. The music is inviting, and I feel I missed out the other night. I've thrown the rugs back, so how about joining me in a dance? Last time you danced more on my feet than on your own—wouldn't you like to rectify that situation?'

Almost against her will, Rowan moved into his arms, and as their steps moved in unison, and their bodies caught the gentle rhythm, she felt again the disturbing and wonderfully joyous experience of being caught and held in a beam of light. It flowed through her, over her, causing in her a golden bubbling sense of breathtaking exhilaration. She revelled in it, and wanted it to go on forever, yet it scared her, because she knew that the more Drew's arms were about her, the more she wanted him to hold her. She felt his breath in her hair, his cheek against hers hard and firm, and she knew she was being foolish, but was helpless to break away. She loved to dance and he was an excellent partner. Where would it end?—oh, don't let it end!

Suddenly they were thrust apart by Khan who had become jealous of their closeness and they both ended up laughing and consoling him for being so neglected. Was Drew as relieved as she was that Khan had brought the delightful interlude to such an abrupt halt? She thought so, because he was careful not to meet her eyes as they walked out to the station-wagon in the gathering dusk, with Khan sharing his affection equally between them.

Stars came out in the velvet-blue carpet of the sky as they drove towards Collingwood, and a huge orange moon hung in the heavens, so big that it looked like a studio prop. Must have been a full-moon madness which had kept them dancing for hours when it felt like only minutes.

'Do you want Khan inside or out? He'll sleep happily on the end of your bed if you'll permit, but I must warn you he takes up more than his share,' Drew asked as they reached the back door.

'Oh, I'll keep him inside with me,' Rowan said,

laughing up into Drew's face. 'Will you come in for coffee?'

'No, better not. I'll pick you up about ten tomorrow morning. We'll go to Canaan.' He was smiling.

'The promised land?' Rowan laughed a little breathlessly.

'Just that, but we won't spend forty years in the wilderness, that's a promise. I'll have to be back to milk the cows.'

'Can I help again tomorrow night?'

'No. Jordan's mother will be home.'

Disappointment swamped her suddenly and it must have shown in her blue eyes, because his smile disappeared and for a timeless moment they gazed at each other, then his arms came round her and his lips met hers, and the night and the trees seemed to enfold them . . . and the light, the marvellous light.

When he lifted his head, that curious, unreadable expression was back in his eyes. 'Go inside. I'll see you in the morning.' He reached round behind her and opened the door and thrust her none too gently inside, pushing Khan in with her. 'Take good care of her, Khan. Guard, on guard.'

She stood listening for the sound of the car fading down the hill and bent down to stroke Khan's thick coat. 'Poor boy. There's a good fellow. I miss him too. You'll have to make do with my company, I'm afraid. I'll see if there's anything you could fancy in the fridge.'

As she sipped her coffee and Khan chewed on a few left-overs, she envied his ability to be satisfied with mere food. She knew from that last kiss that there was no turning back the tide, she had fallen in love with Drew Hewitt, and she wanted to be in his company all the time, twenty-four hours a day, or more. Oh, what a fool! Could it be just rebound? He was madly attractive, and she did miss Greg, but only a little . . . not devastatingly.

Oh, and she missed Drew, *devastatingly*.

She showered and changed into a silk nightgown and lay in bed going over the day in her mind. She must keep remembering that Drew didn't fancy marriage, not even to Regan. He only offered it as an option coupled with a quick divorce. Marriage wasn't in his scheme of things. And she had decided against any attachments until she had the wisdom to make a good judgment of character. But now, this very moment, having only spent one day with Drew, she wanted him for keeps.

It wasn't on . . . it just wasn't on. He was just minding her to protect Regan. For sure he was attracted to her, but most unwillingly. And those kisses? Were they just supposed to keep her entertained and docile until Regan got back? Or just one-upmanship against Jordan? She knew so little—only that she loved being with him. It took her ages to get to sleep, but it was comforting to have Khan lying quietly at the bottom of the bed. At least she had something of Drew's near her.

In the early hours of the morning she was woken by Khan's furious barking out in the kitchen, then as she sat up in bed rubbing the sleep from her eyes, he came bounding in and, paws up on the window-sill, he growled deep in his throat. His hair was standing on end, his teeth were bared, and he looked a ferocious beast.

She slipped out of bed to look out on to the lawn and saw Jordan standing there. The moonlight made it as bright as day, silvering his hair and outlining his face and body in a golden glow. Talk about a young Greek god, she thought, and giggled. He was angry and yelling at Khan, who was reciprocating with savage barks.

'Shut up, the pair of you. Be quiet, Khan. *Sit*.' Khan immediately sat, tense and watchful, his eyes on Jordan. Rowan realised that if she could see every detail of Jordan's clothing, he likewise could see her, so she quickly stretched out her hand for her robe.

'I like you better without it,' Jordan offered with a grin.

'What do you mean by coming here at this time of night?' she demanded. 'Are you crazy?'

'Not as crazy as you are. What do you mean by having that brute in your room? He's a menace. Drew ought to have him put down.' Jordan's voice became gentler. 'I only want to talk to you.'

'Come back in the morning,' Rowan suggested.

'And find you gone? I called half a dozen times yesterday. Where were you?'

'I went out for a picnic with Drew.'

'With Drew!' He spat the words out. 'Look, open the window so I can talk to you.'

'No, thanks. Come back in the morning.'

'Open the window or *I* will. These are the old push-up sort. They don't lock.' When she didn't move he stepped forward to lift the bottom section and Khan lunged for him, barking menacingly.

'*Sit*,' Rowan commanded, and Khan obeyed her like a lamb while she pulled the window down again. She felt thrilled that such a massive dog as Khan would do her bidding, and hugged him. 'You gorgeous thing.'

He twisted his head out of her embrace to keep his eye on the fuming Jordan.

'So big brother Drew feels like cutting himself a slice of the action, does he? Well, he can forget it. I saw you first.'

Rowan laughed. 'Do you two play finders keepers with your girl-friends?'

'Don't think it's funny. He's like a mother hen clucking over one chick with Regan. But he's not going to be *your* cuddly blanket.'

Rowan smiled. 'And how do you propose to stop him?'

'You get rid of that dog or I'll do it for you. Drew trained him on me—you might say he literally cut his back teeth on me. I thought it was funny at the time, he was only a puppy, but now he's the size of a horse he's a different proposition. Regan dotes on him, too.'

'I thought Regan doted on *you*, too. Or is that one of the lies you enjoy telling?'

'It's no lie—you ask her when you meet her. Regan loves me.'

'Well, why be selfish? Doesn't Drew need someone to love him?'

'Don't tell me you're volunteering for that futile position. Drew doesn't love anybody but himself and his farm. Girls always throw themselves at him, but they come unstuck. He's a friend of all and master of none. I think he's taken the vow of celibacy, so be warned. You'll have more fun with me, anyway.'

'I might at that,' Rowan agreed. 'Come back in the daytime and we'll talk about it.'

'I'll be here in the morning,' Jordan promised. 'Early.'

'Don't bother. Make it Wednesday. I'm going out with Drew all day tomorrow.'

'You're showing very poor taste. He's *boring*. I'll be back Wednesday . . . don't make any plans. Mind if I borrow your car to get myself home?'

'As long as you bring it back in one piece,' Rowan told him. There wasn't much else she could say. She had left the keys in it and she had a feeling he would borrow it, anyway. At least it would get him away.

'Goodnight, sweet dreams.' Jordan blew her a kiss and disappeared.

As Rowan climbed back into bed, she shivered. Imagine if he had come calling and she hadn't had Khan to protect her. Once more she owed Drew a debt of gratitude. Sure, she could have handled him this time because she wasn't drugged, but it would have been a battle. Khan had settled it quickly, and Rowan smiled as she saw the big dog sitting watching the window, his head turning to follow the sound of the car engine going downhill, before relaxing and taking up his former position.

If Jordan wanted to be friends and escort her about, she would accept his offer. It would camouflage her real feelings for Drew. That way he wouldn't know she had been fool enough to fall in love with him. Jordan had confirmed Drew's previous statement about remaining a bachelor. It would be too embarrassing to be given the brush-off like the rest of the girls who had fallen for him. He sounded a real Casanova, and with his looks, no wonder he attracted the girls. With that thought, she snuggled down to sleep.

Next morning Drew arrived exactly at ten. Rowan was ready and waiting, dressed in a silky, very feminine sundress with flaring skirt and thin bootlace straps, and pretty sandals. She smiled as she got into the car behind the eager Khan. She liked a man who was punctual. She liked Drew, and her pleasure showed on her glowing face.

'Good morning! Have a good night's sleep?' There was a twinkle in his eye. 'Or did you have a prowler—?'

'How did you know?' she demanded in surprise.

'Well, when I saw your Mazda at home this morning I knew Jordan had come calling. Did Khan greet him enthusiastically?'

'You knew that would happen!' she accused him.

'I knew it could happen—not *would*.'

'Where's Canaan?' She pushed Khan away laughing. He was so excited, leaning forward from the back seat, his fine head thrust between the two of them, loving first one and then the other.

'Down, Khan.' The big dog nuzzled Drew one more time before casting himself down on the back seat, a contented, smiling look in his golden eyes.

Rowan hoped she wasn't giving *herself* away so obviously.

'We got almost to the top of Takaha Hill then turn off,

but I've decided to take you through the Ngarua Caves first. They're just a few miles farther on. There are many caves in New Zealand, but not any to compare with the beauty and atmosphere that you'll see here. They're about twenty to forty feet below the surface, extremely well-lit—I'm sure you'll enjoy it.'

'I'm not sure I like going underground.'

'You'll be quite safe. I'll be with you,' he said, as if that settled the matter.

Once inside, Rowan agreed with him. It was perfectly safe and incredibly beautiful. Fantastic hues of biscuit, fawn, gold and white were highlighted by well-appointed electric lighting, and the stalagmites and stalactites lined the walls, floor and ceilings, creating an effect of a mysterious fairyland.

The guide showed them shapes and interesting forms like pipe organs, dancers, butterflies, golfballs and candles and even politicians, but the highlight was the main cavity in the cave called the Cathedral Dome. Rowan would have loved to return some day when there was a group of schoolchildren singing there. Apparently the sound was magnificent, as the dome formation created perfect acoustics.

Out in the brilliant sunshine again, Drew showed her a view of Tasman Bay and D'Urville Island before heading back to a turn-off right at the top of the range and, driving along a terribly narrow gravel road, pointed to wonderfully unusual and grotesque marble outcrops.

'We'll pull in here. See that timber-truck crawling up in low gear towards us? This is a tough enough road without us making it more difficult for him. We'll eat our picnic when we get through the Canaan tablelands, as there's a good picnic spot among the beech forest, then we'll walk into Harwood's Hole. It's the deepest known Southern Hemisphere chasm, twelfth deepest in the world.'

'Sounds sinister. Have you a deep motive for taking me there, if you'll pardon the pun?'

Drew laughed, 'Now that you come to mention it, that could solve all our problems. Trouble is, a lot of cavers spend time down there. You'd be discovered very quickly.'

'Or my bones,' Rowan said with a realistic shudder. She watched nervously as the heavily-laden timber-truck inched past them, wondering if the towering load was going to crush them into the mountainside. 'Anyway, Jordan would raise the alarm. He's taking me out tomorrow.'

'He is not,' Drew informed her flatly. 'You agreed that you'd only be seen with me until Regan gets back.'

'Oh, I forgot about that. Honestly I did. Now he'll be angry with me.'

'How unfortunate,' Drew sounded quite pleased. 'You can ring him when we get back.'

He drove on with such a contented expression on his tanned face that Rowan wanted to jolt him in some way. As he parked in a natural clearing in the native forest she helped him unpack lunch, then asked, 'Why does Jordan see you as a confirmed bachelor? Owning all that land, I thought you'd be bound to marry and have an heir to carry on. What's the point in working all your life if you can't hand it on to someone?'

'Jordan knows I can't marry. How could I bring a wife into that house, with him and his mother there? They'd destroy any chance I had of making a wife happy.'

If she had hoped to ruffle him, she failed. Drew stretched out comfortably with a mug of tea in one hand and an enormous sandwich in the other, but his grey eyes were alert, waiting for her reaction.

Rowan brushed her hair back from her face, before taking her own tea. 'You mean you'd let Jordan and his mother dictate to you. You disappoint me. The night I met you, all the men were congratulating you on your skill at manoeuvring the government into a position where they had to grant this district some concessions. Don't tell me the politicians are a soft touch!'

'No, I won't tell you that, but they are open to reason and my two partners are not. Mrs Hewitt the second is a very determined and spiteful woman and she is dedicating her life to frustrating mine.'

'And you accept that!' Rowan's blue eyes widened in astonishment.

'Not with good grace,' Drew smiled at her. 'You could call it a stalemate. You see we have equal voting rights. Jordan plays us off one against the other—it amuses him. He won't vote with her to sell the farm, which drives her demented, but neither will he vote with me to build another house on the property so that I can have a separate establishment. So we all live together in a crooked little house.'

'How horrible. How will it end?'

'We all have our own ideas on that. For myself, I'll play the waiting game. I've got as much determination as the rest of them and, I hope, more patience.'

'But what happens if Jordan wants to marry? Will you be nasty and make him bring his bride home to live—?'

'It could depend on who she is.' His eyes gleamed.

'It sounds as if it could be Regan,' Rowan suggested.

'Wait till you meet Regan.'

'I *am* waiting,' Rowan said impatiently. 'You're not very helpful, but Regan will tell me everything.'

His eyes lit with laughter. 'You know, I think you could be right about that. I think Regan is going to like you very much.'

'Oh, do you really think so?' Rowan knew she was being side-tracked, but she longed to talk about her twin. 'When did you discover I wasn't Regan?'

Drew helped himself to another sandwich. 'Well, I left

you at the motor camp and went off to find Jordan.' He paused, then with a rueful smile added, 'He irritated me somewhat and I lost my temper, so gained little information but much satisfaction by landing one on him. I drove home to change and think what I'd do, and saw the lights on at the McKinnons'. I decided that as Daniel had already missed Regan, I'd better let him know she was okay. You can't imagine how I felt when I walked in and found Regan there. It was unbelievable. She had had a stomach upset, and it was obvious from their conversation that she'd been home all night. I waited until she went back to bed, then told Daniel about you. He sort of went white around the gills and announced he was going to bed, so there I was, none the wiser. Oh, he knew more than he was telling and, as I went out, asked me not to say anything to Regan until he had had a chance to talk to her.'

'And?' Rowan prompted anxiously.

Maddeningly relaxed, Drew poured himself another cup of tea, chose a thick slice of fruit cake and settled back.

'What happened then? Oh, do stop eating and tell me.'

'This is a picnic. At picnics you are supposed to eat.' He laughed at her furious face.

'You're just teasing me. I *want* to know. Don't you see?—if he was upset and rushed her away, it means that he hasn't told her she's adopted. This holiday wasn't planned, was it?' Rowan got to her feet and stood over him in a threatening manner. 'I'll push you into Harwood's Hole when we get there if you don't answer me!'

'Resorting to violence won't get you anywhere. You played a trick on me, pretending to be Regan. Try a bit of this cake, it's very good.' He took another bite with great satisfaction.

Fuming, she watched him demolish the cake. 'And how long are you going to make me wait?'

'I don't know,' he teased with a provoking grin. 'It

would be sooner if you'd stop threatening me and were *very* nice to me.'

'How nice?' Rowan's eyes narrowed dangerously.

'Oh, not *that* nice,' he returned hastily. 'I'm not Jordan. Just clear the picnic remains up if you've finished. You've got a very poor appetite, I must say.'

A glorious blush stained Rowan's cheeks as she flung the picnic remains into the basket. He had meant her to misunderstand. The very nuance in his voice had directed her to jump to that conclusion. Smart Drew Hewitt . . . she'd love to push him down the twelfth deepest hole in the world. Then again, she'd hate to drive out on that terrifying road on her own. In silence she tidied up the rubbish then, hands on hips, eyed him tensely.

'Are you going to tell me now?'

'Of course.' His smile was disarming. 'I drove back to the Camping Ground, but you'd disappeared, which made me very tetchy indeed. I had been very concerned about you . . .'

'Only because you thought I was Regan,' she interrupted savagely.

'Of course. But you improve with knowing, so if a similar situation arose, I just might bestir myself enough to rescue you for your own sweet sake.'

Knowing she was being got at did nothing to cool Rowan's temper. 'You're more than kind.'

'I know. Don't you find I improve with knowing?'

'Not at all.'

'Pity. However, I'll put you out of your misery. I got back to the farm and Daniel came hurrying over to say he had to make an urgent trip away and could I handle his farm for a couple of days. He gave me a few instructions and off he went.'

'You mean you never actually talked to Regan. You don't know *anything*!'

'I know quite a lot that you'd give your eye-teeth for,

young Rowan, and if you hope to get close to Regan you'd better keep on my good side. Daniel trusts me, he doesn't trust Jordan, and with very good reason. If you want to talk to McKinnon, then I'll have to vouch for you. Come along now, you'll have to step it out if we're going to get to the Hole and back home in time for milking.'

Grimly she realised he was speaking the truth and started to follow him through the forest, watching for the blazed trail.

Over his shoulder he asked, 'What are you going to be doing tomorrow, now that you're not going out with Jordan? I could pick you up at ten . . .'

'Don't bother. I'm going to be spending the day with Rochelle, my next-door neighbour. I promised to take the kids off her for a day so that she could catch up on her sleep.'

'Very commendable.' Laughter lilted his words. 'I'll come and give you a hand.'

She wanted to tell him that she never wanted to see him again, but it would have been a lie. 'You will let me know the minute the McKinnons are back?'

'You have my word.'

The track got steeper and he turned often to give her a helping hand, and slowly her anger faded away. She had his word and she would rather take his word than anyone's, except her own parents'. He wasn't a man to go back on a promise, she knew that instinctively, the same way that she knew she was enjoying this day in his company more than she had ever enjoyed any other day in her life.

When Drew dropped her off with Khan late in the afternoon he came into the kitchen with her. 'Sure you won't change your mind and come out with me tomorrow? I don't mind if you bring the children.'

Rowan was sorely tempted. Tomorrow would seem quite dull without getting a view of Drew. 'No, I can't do that. It wouldn't be fair to Jordan. He asked me first, and if I can't go with him, I can't go with you.'

'He won't play fair with you,' Drew told her.

'That's his problem, not mine. Thank you for a lovely day.'

'Seems I can't shake you, so I'll be off. I've enjoyed the day, too. Sure you've got all you need?'

'There are a few things I need from the store. Is it all right for me to go down there?'

'Certainly not. I don't want you going anywhere. Give me a list, and I'll shoot down now and get them for you. I'll put them in your milk box by the garage at the foot of the hill.'

He took a note of her needs and, refusing any money, drove off. Rowan walked through to the front verandah, and wondered why she felt slightly let down at the way he had rushed off. He could have . . . well perhaps not . . . not in broad daylight. Disconsolately, she sat on the step looking out at the Bay. It really was a delightful spot. She loved the small point of land jutting out into the water. It looked so perfect; the huge spreading trees, the neat patch of lawn, bright caravans and tents and the neat white fence by the boating ramp. Wapping Point would look wonderful on a postcard. She must get some to post to her parents. They would love to see the Pupu Springs, the Ngarua Caves and Harwood's Hole, and the tablelands of Canaan. Maybe they could come and stay with her, always providing she herself was able to stay after tomorrow.

'Free delivery service.'

Khan was barking excitedly as he welcomed Drew back, and as Rowan stood up to greet him, her eyes were shining. 'I thought you were leaving them in the box.'

'They were too heavy for you to lug up the hill. Actually, I felt I had disappointed Khan by not saying farewell in the appropriate manner.'

Rowan felt her pulses racing as he stepped towards her. 'It would be awful to disappoint Khan,' she said softly.

'I knew you'd agree with me.' He bent swiftly and kissed her once, and once again. 'When you establish a good precedent it's criminal to neglect to take advantage of it. Goodbye, Rowan. Stay, Khan.'

And then he was gone from sight. Rowan leaned against the verandah post, her vivid blue eyes dreamy and soft, her finger outlining her mouth as if in wonder at the ecstasy that swept through her each time Drew's lips were on hers. That a man could make her feel so full of longing and desire that she would count everyone else in the world well lost, if only she could be with him all the time—even her own parents whom she loved so dearly. Should she have to choose between seeing him or seeing them, there would be no contest. Was this the divine spark that her father had spoken of? This radiance within, this boundless joy, this true delight of spirit and soul, and it hardly mattered that he had not even spoken of love. Even if he never did, she would still be thrilled that she had experienced such a depth of emotion, such an affinity with another human being that her ordinary world was shattered and would never be the same again.

Drew Hewitt! She bent to hug Khan. 'I love him, Khan, just like you do. But he loves you back, and he's only using me. And I didn't even know he existed four days ago. How could something so tremendous happen in such a short time?'

She had to ring Jordan and she wanted to put off the evil moment. How could he understand? She hadn't confided in him that she was Regan's twin, or that she would slip away without contacting Regan, if that was necessary. Loving Drew made that decision a million times harder.

Rowan walked quickly to the phone, determined to get it over with. She would ring before Drew got home, and she hoped that Jordan would answer.

'Jordan Hewitt speaking.'

Rowan smiled. Even over the telephone wires you could feel his impudence and almost see his smile. 'Rowan here, Jordan. I'm ringing to say I can't go out with you tomorrow. I do apologise . . .'

'But owing to unforeseen circumstances,' he interrupted harshly. 'I gather Drew, my beloved brother, has something to do with your decision. It's amazing the power he has to addle the brains of quite intelligent females. What yarn did he spin you?'

'None really, and I have apologised. You see, I feel it's better that I'm not seen around until Regan comes home. I don't want to make life difficult for her.'

'I thought you'd just spent the day with Drew! Were you invisible?'

'Almost,' Rowan said with a giggle. 'You know that if anyone saw me with him they would take me for Regan, so there's no harm done. If I'm seen with you, they'd know I wasn't Regan.'

'I think you have led a very dull life and are trying to get a bit of drama out of this situation,' Jordan said sarcastically. 'Explain in plain English why it would matter a toss whether you were recognised as Regan or Regan's double?'

'I can't.'

'Or won't!' he said savagely. 'But I bet you confided in darling Drew.'

Rowan felt incredibly guilty. She truly didn't mean to offend Jordan, quite the reverse. If she was staying here, she needed him to camouflage her interest in Drew. 'You're right, of course. I did confide in Drew, but then he's proved himself trustworthy. You, on your own admission, are a confirmed liar and breaker of promises. How can I tell you something confidential?'

Suddenly Jordan laughed. 'Tell you what, I'll take you fishing tonight instead of taking you out tomorrow. It will be dark, and no one will see us. How about that for a compromise?'

'Oh, Jordan, you really are a trappy player. Tell you what, if you ask Drew and he approves, I'll go with you. I'd love to. But Drew has to give me the okay himself.'

'You mean I'm to ask Drew's permission to take you out. You've got to be joking!' He slammed down the receiver.

Rowan laughed as she prepared herself a meal. She felt she had come out of it not too badly. At least she had managed to convey that she'd enjoy an evening's fishing with him. If his pride got in the road of asking Drew's permission, then Jordan could hardly blame her. Quite machiavellian! She was getting as crafty as those two brothers.

A couple of hours later the phone rang and she hurried to answer it.

'Jordan here, Rowan my sweet. Wrap up warmly, put on strong comfortable shoes, you're going fishing.'

'Drew agreed to it!' she exclaimed in surprise.

'Worse than that, he's coming too. Pick you up in an hour. The tide should be on the turn then.'

With a singing heart, Rowan ran to change into jeans and a warm jersey. She was going to spend the evening with Drew and the very thought melted her bones. She would have to be very careful, Jordan was dangerously perceptive and Drew himself was no slouch, but she would risk anything for a few hours more in Drew's company.

She waited an hour and it went past so slowly that the tension built up and up until it was almost unbearable. She wished she could expend her energy somehow, but she wasn't allowed down the beach for a run or a swim. After tomorrow it could be different, she could go anywhere, or she would be leaving Golden Bay altogether.

It was dark now and the tide was running out fast. She hadn't asked where they were going, but it had something to do with the tides. Why didn't they hurry? She decided it was safe to go down to the main road and wait. It was not necessary to call Khan—he never left her side. If she moved from one room to another he got up with lazy grace and stalked after her; if she stood he stood, if she sat down, he did too, thrusting his elegant head on to her lap to be caressed and loved.

Drew's station wagon pulled up just as she reached the milk box. 'Hello again.' He reached back, opening the rear door for Rowan and Khan.

'Hello to you both.' She sat forward, her arm along the back of the front seat resting against Drew's broad shoulders as if accidentally. Dear God, how weak she was, and how deceitful, but it was worth it. His closeness sent her senses reeling.

'As you see, I had to bring my elderly chaperon with me.' Jordan turned in his seat to watch her bright face. 'It's nice to see that you were impatient for my company.'

Rowan laughed. 'I could hardly contain myself. Where are we going?'

'That's how I like my women, warm and eager. We're just going down to Wapping Point, and we'll row across the river, then walk up the mud flats as the tide retreats, fish for an hour or so then, as it comes in again, we'll move fairly hastily to get back here before getting drowned. There's a deep hole out there with loads of fish. Even Drew should catch one or two, but an expert like me should bag about twenty.'

As they parked by the loading ramp, she saw the flicker of amusement in Drew's eyes. Was he as happy as she was?

'Hop in, Rowan, and that mongrel can swim—I'm not wasting my valuable efforts giving him a free ride,' Jordan ordered.

Rowan climbed into the small dinghy which rocked violently, and sat close to Drew who seemed content to let

Jordan take charge of the oars. Khan watched the pro-
ceedings with his head on one side, ears pricked forward,
and as they pulled from the ramp plunged in and swam
strongly behind them.

'Admire my effortless style, Rowan,' Jordan told her
cheerfully. 'This is a tricky piece of navigation with the
current running fast. Unless I hear continuous murmurs
of praise and admiration I may dump you all in the tide.'

'You're wonderful, so handsome, so strong, so cour-
ageous, so modest,' Rowan encouraged him cheerfully,
honestly impressed with his ability.

'I know,' Jordan grinned audaciously. 'Everybody says
so.'

When they pulled the boat up they each carried their
own fishing rod and bait and started walking across the
sand at a fast pace. It was hard slogging, sometimes in
sand, sometimes in mud, and after sloshing through
hundreds of small streams, Rowan protested, 'You said a
mile, we must be nearly to Nelson. I'll never make it back
to the boat when the tide turns.'

'You'll be drowned if you don't,' Jordan said callously.
'I won't be able to carry you, I'll have too many fish, and
Drew can't—he's too old and frail. You're on your own.'

Rowan and Drew laughed with him, and it was only
then that Rowan realised that tonight the atmosphere
between the brothers lacked malice. They were both
enjoying themselves, and she sensed that they had often
done this trip together in happier times. As they reached
the deep hole and baited the hooks her spirits soared,
suddenly carefree and happy, she knew that she was seeing
these two men as they should always be; their cheerful
rivalry and outrageous boasting made the trip hilarious.

Jordan had chosen his night well and the snapper and
bream flung themselves at the bait in a most satisfactory
way. Naturally the men caught the most, but Rowan was
well pleased with her haul. She was no good at unhooking

the fish or baiting the line, so each time she triumphed she had to go to Drew or Jordan for help, and she made sure she alternated her request with meticulous care. She had no intention of being the one to spoil this amazing interlude by being a bone of contention. By the light of the moon she admired the fantastic beauty of the fish, their scales shining iridescent, soft pink and purple and silver, like mother-of-pearl.

They stayed too long, loth to break away, and consequently the tide was rising fast around them as they hurried homeward, tired, breathless but still laughing. Safely back across the dark swift river, Rowan decided against inviting them up for supper. The truce was too fragile a thing to prolong indefinitely.

'Let me off here at the milk box. It's awkward turning at the top, and Khan will see me home safely.'

'Hey! Don't we even get a goodnight kiss apiece for entertaining you so lavishly and at such great expense?' Jordan protested.

'You do not,' Rowan said, getting out of the car with alacrity when Drew braked at the foot of the hill. Once safely on her own two feet, she thanked them. 'It was a wonderful experience. I loved every minute of it, and never have I been escorted by two such charming and handsome men. Thank you. And I don't want to see either of you tomorrow until you bring me news of Regan. Goodnight.' She turned and ran up the hill with Khan at her side.

She heard them jeering from behind her. 'Never even offered to gut the fish!'

'Thankless wench, we won't take her again, not even one measly goodnight kiss!'

She laughed, *that* was Jordan. Drew had already had his kiss, and she imagined his complacent smile. Her life must have been so dull before she met these two, and she hadn't even noticed it. Please God, don't let it all end tomorrow.

CHAPTER SIX

EARLY next morning Rowan with Khan climbed the hill to Rochelle's house, and as she waited for her knock to be answered she heard the sound of the children squabbling and grizzling.

Rochelle's eyes lit with pleasure as soon as she saw them. 'Welcome. Come in if you dare, my place looks as if it's been hit by an atom bomb, not quite demolished, but you wish it had been. How are you? Coffee?'

'Sure,' Rowan told Khan to wait on the verandah and followed her hostess inside. She bent to pick up the wailing Hannah on the way to a chair. 'What's the matter, darling?'

'Cwash down,' the honey-blonde said with large, tear-ful, appealing eyes.

'Did you indeed crash down? I'll hug you better.'

'Me too, hug me, too,' Aaron said anxiously.

'Of course. Hop up on my other knee. Wasn't I lucky God gave me two knees, one for each of you.'

'I wish he'd given me two heads,' Rochelle muttered as she placed a steaming mug of coffee in front of Rowan. 'That way I would have had the brains to know I couldn't cope with two toddlers single-handed. I've reached rock-bottom, energy-wise, confidence-wise and any other wise you'd like to mention. Do you know what I have achieved this morning? I've been up since five and I have the washing on the line. That's it. That's the sum total.'

Rowan smiled at her despairing face. 'Well, that's why I'm here. I am giving you the whole day off. I've got nothing to do, and I'm not allowed to be seen in public, and Regan is due in tonight, so I'm tensed up like a coiled spring. If I haven't got something to use up that tension, I'll explode.'

'You really mean it, don't you?' Rochelle ran her hand through her tumbled red curls. 'I haven't even had time to do my hair this morning. I'm such a mess.'

'I really mean it.' Rowan laughed. 'Look, the kids have taken to me because they think I'm Regan, so there's no problems. I'm used to kids, I love them. As soon as you finish that coffee, you're to go down to my house, throw yourself on a spare bed and sleep the day away. If you wake up before nightfall, I recommend a long hot bath, a meal and watch TV or read some magazines. Come back at six, you'll find the kids bathed and fed and in bed. Howzat!'

'Sounds like my birthday, Christmas, and Mother's Day rolled into one. I accept because I'm too weak-minded to refuse. The kids have a nap after lunch sometimes . . . Oh, I feel awful! I haven't even asked after your progress. I was dying to pop in the last couple of days, but thought it would look too nosey. Anyway, your car was out whenever I passed. Did you find out whether Regan knows she's adopted or not?'

'No. I'll find out tonight. Drew is going to ring me. That's why I'm so keyed up. If she doesn't know then I'll be leaving tonight, so this is your only chance to make use of me. If she does know and I decide to stay for a few months, we'll talk about your nursing offer while I mind the kids.'

'I think I'm too excited to sleep now,' Rochelle said. 'Second thoughts, I'm not. I hate to leave you with this mess . . .'

'Would you be offended if I make myself at home and do the dishes and take a duster around?'

'I give you permission to offend me that way whenever you get the urge.' Rochelle gave her an eloquent glance, then burst into tears. 'You really are an answer to prayer . . .'

'No more talking. Out! Pick up a change of clothes before you go. Use my smellies, they're in the bathroom, and anything else you fancy. Now be off.'

The day passed remarkably quickly. The children were impossibly good, Aaron showing her where the vacuum cleaner was and cleaning detergents and pointing out any dirt he felt she had overlooked, while Hannah burbled around, tripping over the electrolux cord, removing pots and pans from the cupboards and muttering 'Cwashed down' whenever in need of a cuddle. They both loved Khan, and he tolerated them with unbelievable patience, because Rowan said he must, but now and again gave her a reproachful look to show that dogs of his vastly aristocratic lineage weren't supposed to be clambered over and dribbled on.

When Rochelle returned she found the house neat and tidy, windows sparkling and two very tired children bathed, fed and dressed for bed.

'How did you do it? The place looks fantastic and the kids look lovable again.'

'They always were, you were just too tired to see it. You do look wonderfully refreshed.'

'I am, quite relaxed and sanity restored. I slept till three, lay in the bath for hours reading a book, something I love doing, and I feel a new woman.'

'Good. Will you put the kids down? They're exhausted because they decided to help me instead of having a nap, so they should sleep well. I'll dish up your meal, then I'll be off in case Drew rings.'

'Just ring the exchange and tell them you're up here.' Rochelle let the children kiss Rowan goodnight, then shepherded them ahead of her to the bedroom. When she returned she took her place at the table and beamed at Rowan. 'What a pleasure to sit down to a meal I haven't cooked. I haven't been bothering much lately, just picking at what the kids don't want. I'm going to turn over a new leaf, because I shouldn't have let myself get so low.'

Rowan looked at her sympathetically. 'Caring for two kids solo is a pretty lonely road. I think you've done wonderfully well. The children are really delightful.'

'What can I say to thank you?'

'Nothing. I told you I had to use up that excess energy or burst.'

'I saw Drew's car outside a couple of times. Do you like him any better now you've got to know him?'

Rowan thought how she had stormed up the hill, breathless with rage, the last time she visited Rochelle, and giggled. 'I don't want to murder him any more . . . well, only now and again.'

'And Jordan?' Rochelle asked with a smile. 'Did you forgive him?'

'Oh, stop looking so smug because you've been proved right. Yes, I forgave Jordan. They're most unusual, those two brothers, or is that just me?'

'No, it's not just you. They are exceptionally nice. I don't have much to do with them, but the district thinks they're pretty special. Well, they would do, they're both star rugby players and Golden Bay lives for its rugby. If you're here in the winter you'll know what I mean. The whole community turns out to support their home games and there's a mass migration when they play away. Drew and Jordan play completely different games, the way they choose different life-styles; but what they do, they do well.'

'What *does* Jordan do well? I know Drew does the farm, but Jordan told me he never works.'

Rochelle laughed. 'He doesn't call it work. Well, my wood-shed is never empty. That's Jordan. He just takes off with a power-saw and lands up here with a trailer-load of wood. You can't pay him. He does it for others, too—pensioners, you know. And he'll spend days fishing or whitebaiting and then give it all away. That garage at your place, for instance. He found a huge rimu tree swept down in a flood and landed over the other side of the river. He couldn't bear not to use it, so got a chain-saw and took off the roots and branches, sawed it in half and waited for high tide, then floated it down to the Point about half a mile. He cut it up at low tide, and then nearly lost it in a flood again, and sat there all night keeping it safe.'

Rowan looked at her in astonishment. 'But that's *work*!'

'Hard work,' Rochelle confirmed. 'Then he got a front-end loader and had it carted to the sawmill at Bainham. He worked for the owner for two weeks and got the logs sawn into timber, and built that garage. No money changed hands, it's not Jordan's way. If ever a war comes and we're cut off from supplies, I hope I'm living near him. He knows this country backwards; where to catch fish, shoot deer or goats, find gold or coal. Don't be fooled by Jordan, he's got more clues than most.'

Rowan looked at her thoughtfully. 'Thanks for telling me, not that I ever did underestimate him. What's his mother like?'

Rochelle grimaced. 'Hardly my cup of tea, but then, I'm definitely not hers either. She is an extremely good-looking woman—very tall, slim, expensively dressed whenever I see her, and has the coldest most calculating eyes I've ever seen. Still, most people seem to get on okay with her, but she gives Drew a hard time. I hear she was all over him when she and his father first married, but as soon as Jordan was born she turned on him and made his life hell. Poor kid, he got away as soon as he could, but when his father died he had to come back and live in the same house. It can't be easy.'

The phone rang stridently, and Rowan leapt to her feet. 'That will be my call.'

'Probably, go ahead and answer it.'

'That you, Rowan? Drew here. I have good news and bad news, which do you want first?'

Rowan went tense. 'The bad.'

'When Daniel arrived home he was on his own. Regan is still away, so you won't be able to see her.'

'And the good news?'

'She does know she's adopted, so you're quite okay to stay here . . .'

'Oh, Drew, how splendid. I'm so relieved. Thank you for ringing me, and thank you for speaking to Mr McKinnon. He probably would have set his dogs on me.'

'Think nothing of it. Are you going to stay on then?'

She was sorely tempted to ask if he wanted her to, but decided against it. It would be awful to sustain a 'Crash down' after such good news. 'Of course I am. I'll stay until Regan comes home.'

'That may be quite a while according to Daniel,' Drew warned her.

'However long it takes, I'm waiting.' Rowan said cheerfully. 'She *is* coming back someday?'

'Definitely. Listen to me, Rowan. I think Jordan may be headed your way. I hope he is. He's had a bit of a shock, and God only knows what he'll do. It will either be to you or towards the pub; as I said, I hope he'll unload his troubles on to you. Go and tie Khan up, I left a chain and collar under the pear tree. I'd hate Khan to take a piece out of him today.'

'You sound really concerned. Is it serious?'

'When Jordan's in a rage it's usually serious, if not for him, for anyone who gets in his road. I tried to talk to him, but he stormed off.'

'I'm at Rochelle's. I'll go straight home and tie Khan. He's not going to be pleased with me.'

'He'll get over it. Listen, Rowan, you will be kind to Jordan, will you?'

'How kind?' Rowan asked nervously.

'Not *that* kind,' Drew snapped. 'Give me a ring when he leaves.'

Again Rowan was tempted to say something stupid like 'if he leaves', but thought better of it. She could hear the anxiety in Drew's voice. 'Okay.'

She hung up, said goodbye to Rochelle after hurriedly telling her the good news, then called Khan and ran for her house. Khan stood very aggrieved as she buckled the collar around his neck and Rowan's heart smote her. 'Sorry, Khan, it's a rotten trick and I'll come and let you go as soon as Jordan leaves, and I'll give you a very special supper. You've been so good with the kids today, I'm sorry to treat you to this.'

She heard the Mazda roaring up the hill as she walked to the back door, and decided to wait and speak to Jordan out of doors. She really had no idea what to expect, but Drew couldn't have told her to tie Khan if he had any worries about Jordan misbehaving himself. She would have loved to enjoy her own good news quietly and then ring her parents, but Drew had asked her. She would do anything for Drew.

'Feel like a night out?' Jordan asked as soon as he sighted her.

'Not really. I was out late fishing with you two last night, and I've looked after Aaron and Hannah all day today. I'm a spent force. What did you have in mind?' She thought Drew was exaggerating Jordan's mood, because he seemed as casual and relaxed as normal, but then she saw the deep anger and resentment in his eyes.

'Nothing much, just a trip to the Rat Trap, a few drinks and a talk. You know, the pub at the foot of Takaka Hill. There'll be the usual crowd there, you could enjoy yourself.'

'I could, but I'd rather just sit on the front verandah and sag a little. You're welcome to join me in the unwinding process, or if you'd rather you can borrow my car.' She watched him, wondering if she had worded her refusal correctly.

His face tightened, 'You know Regan isn't coming home.'

'Yes, Drew rang me. I told him I was going to wait here till she did return. I do want to see her.'

'Not as much as I do.' He bit the words off savagely.

'I suppose not,' Rowan offered with a sympathetic smile. 'Do you mind if we sit down? I'm tired.' She walked towards the front, not knowing if he was going to follow her or not. She sat down, her chin propped on her knees, watching across the Bay, seeing the tide starting to run out. There was something soothing about the perpetual moving in and out of water.

Jordan stalked around the corner, lithe and active like a tiger deprived of its prey. 'You say that so calmly. Do you know how long you'll be waiting for Regan? She's gone abroad indefinitely. Packed up, cleared out without a word. You can wait, but I'm damned if I will.'

Rowan eyed him steadily. 'She's going to come back, Drew said so. Whether you wait or not is your decision.'

'You're right there.' He thrust his hands into his jeans pockets, his stance angry and aggressive. 'And are you going to tell me your deep dark secret? I deserve as much information as Drew has.'

'Certainly. Regan and I are identical twins. I was adopted into one family, she in another. I came looking for her when I found out, but everyone seemed to assume she was the natural daughter of the McKinnons and I thought if she was ignorant of the fact she was adopted, it would hurt her to have it thrust in front of her so brutally. I've been waiting to find out if she was aware of the fact. Drew said she was, so my problem's settled.'

'She never told me she was adopted. I thought you were just a freak double. It does happen.'

'I'm no freak. Watch your words.'

Jordan smiled nastily. 'You're alike in every physical dimension. I don't even have to close my eyes to imagine Regan here. I'll make do with you.'

'*Oh, no, you don't,*' Rowan cried, instinctively jumping to her feet ready for flight.

Jordan laughed harshly and caught her hand, jerking her forward against him roughly, ignoring her protests, his hazel eyes cruel and hard.

'You've been begging for this, my flower, since the first moment we met, so stop pretending. If I needed any proof or encouragement I have it out there in the yard. Why else did you tie Khan up?'

His arms were like steel bands around her, crushing her slim soft body against his with calculated brutality, and she fought against the faintness of pain and shock at the suddenness of his attack. 'You're hurting me,' she gasped in anguish.

'Not as much as I'm going to,' Jordan said savagely. 'I'll teach you and your sweet sister to play tricks on me.'

He caught her hair in his hand and jerked her head back, and despair filled her as she saw the smouldering rage and anger and bitterness in his eyes. Then his lips came down on hers, burning and bruising her mouth with violent intensity, showing no pity, seeking to revenge himself for the loss of Regan. As her senses reeled, she seemed to become one with him in the darkness and pain of his fury, and prayed silently for help, knowing nothing could save her, yet asking just the same.

Then suddenly the punishment stopped and his lips lifted off hers. She knew he was supporting her because she had no strength to stand herself. Thankfulness swept over her, then anger that Drew had let this happen to her. She would never trust him again. She kept her eyes closed, too frightened to look at Jordan, although she knew the moment of madness had passed. She felt the tension leave his body and knew that she herself was limp and drained.

Then Rowan felt his lips brush her eyelids as soft and gentle as a butterfly's wing, then trail across her cheek and tease gently at the corners of her mouth before claiming them in a kiss of surprising tenderness and sweetness. Horrified, she fought her instinct to put her arms around him and comfort him. She realised the kiss was an apology, his way of trying to wipe out the fear and pain he had caused her. Then she tasted the salt of tears on her lips and knew they were his tears and not hers. Vaguely she understood the rage and the terrifying enormity of the gap in his life now that Regan was gone.

'Marry me, Rowan?' His hand brushed her hair away from her face. 'I'll try to make you happy.'

Rowan's blue eyes flew open. 'Marry you! Be a permanent substitute for Regan? *Not likely!* Not even if I was coming out of anaesthetic from a lobotomy operation.' She moved from his arms and sat shakily on the step.

'That's a very emphatic refusal. Why won't you marry me?' He watched her unnervingly.

'How can you ask?' Rowan demanded angrily. 'One, I don't love you. Come to that, I'm not even sure I like you. Two, I wouldn't marry a man I couldn't trust, and you are the most untrustworthy man I've ever met. You lie . . .'

'If I gave you my word always to be honest with you . . . would that change your mind?'

Her blue eyes flashed. '*Nothing* would change my mind. You're a liar and a malicious prankster. You get your kicks upsetting people, playing unfunny jokes. Imagine my taking you home to my family . . . I would have to say that although you'd tell me the truth, you'd lie to them and to all my friends. And what about children . . . ? Children need honesty above everything else, except love. You boast about your lack of integrity as if it was something to be proud of. I'm glad Regan is away. I hope she finds someone decent to love. You're a walking disaster area!'

Jordan took a step towards her menacingly. 'Big words for someone alone, with Khan tied up.'

His meaning was plain, but strangely it did not frighten Rowan. She knew instinctively the danger was past. Why was she bothering to discuss such a farcical idea with him? It felt as if she was fighting him for Regan's sake.

She glared at him. 'You threatening rape again? What would it prove? That you are stronger physically than me! Surely you need more satisfaction from life than that. Or would it ease the rejection you're feeling from Regan leaving you?'

'Something like that . . .' He gave her a curious look as if puzzled by her lack of fear. 'You know she never even rang me, or wrote, and she could be gone for six months or a year? . . . Do you call that loving?'

'Maybe she's tired of loving you . . .'

'Not that. Regan will always love me,' Jordan said fiercely.

'I wouldn't count on it. You see, I know by experience that you can come to the end of love. I loved a guy once, selfish, just like you, and I kept making excuses for him, but once he did something so mean that I stopped loving him right then and there, and I haven't regretted it, not for one moment. I feel free now. Maybe Regan feels free now to . . .'

'*Shut up!*'

'No, I won't shut up. Perhaps this time you went too far. Perhaps she saw that you'd stop at nothing to get your own way. You knew what you were up to, taking me to the dance like that, making fools of the people who were there, ruining her reputation so that her father wouldn't let her go away on that art course. You were so set on having her near you that you were prepared to sacrifice her happiness and her future. Perhaps that was the final straw . . . it must have sickened her, so she went away without a word. She must have known you'd never change.'

Jordan loomed over her, his fist clenched as if to strike her, then he turned away, staring out over the Bay. 'That's not true. I can change if I want to, I just don't want to. Why should I? And Regan will always love me. Nothing you say can alter that.'

But Rowan saw the arrogance and anger slide from him. She could not see his face, but the set of his shoulders told her that her words were having some dramatic effect on him, as if for the first time he was facing the reality that Regan might be finished with him.

'She might always love you, Jordan, but she'll never marry you, not the way you are. A girl wants someone to lean on occasionally, to be proud of—not a comic act. Maybe you can change, maybe you can't. Maybe Regan doesn't mean that much to you, maybe she's not worth the effort. I haven't met her yet, but what I've heard makes me think she's a real person and the man she chooses would have to be a real man, not someone hiding his feelings and insecurities behind a mask of lies and tricks.'

He didn't answer her, just stood gazing out to sea as if carved from stone. She sat silent for a long time, then continued, 'Only you can make the decision, Jordan. How important is she to you? If some other girl would do, then I'd settle for that, because changing your attitude to life won't be easy, and then there's the risk that you've left your run too late. You'd better count the cost before you try. That night at the dance when Drew believed I was Regan, he said people can change, and that he honestly thought you loved her enough to make the effort, and also that she was the only person that ever had any faith in you. That's not true, of course. Drew had faith in you, too.'

'How do you know that?' His voice was gravelly.

'Because he was so angry that you'd pulled another stupid trick. He wouldn't have been mad if he hadn't cared about you. And he still loves you and trusts you. He proved that tonight.'

Jordan swung round and stared at her. 'What makes you say that?'

Rowan fought the tears of her own pain, and swallowed with difficulty. 'Drew told me to tie Khan up. He trusted you not to hurt me. He thought you needed someone to talk to . That's a lot of trust.'

Jordan grinned suddenly. 'And if his faith had been misplaced?'

Rowan did not flinch. 'That's something I'll be taking up with Drew at a later date.'

The smile left his good-looking face. 'Thank you for telling me, Rowan, and for talking to me. Can I borrow your car for a couple of days?'

'If you want to. Where are you going?'

'Up to the mountains to sort myself out. I think better there. I'll see you when I get back.'

'Do that.'

He walked towards the end of the verandah, then turned and said awkwardly, 'Sorry about what happened earlier . . .'

Rowan stood up wearily. 'Forget it, I will.'

'You *are* very like Regan. She doesn't bear grudges either.' He waved and disappeared.

Rowan felt exhausted and made her way slowly to the pear tree and let Khan go. He ran with ferocious snarls towards the garage, but was too late—Jordan was driving safely down the hill. Frustrated, he chased Rochelle's cat up the hill, barking furiously as it scrambled up a tree out of harm's way. Rowan called him off and took him inside to feed him lavishly to soothe his ruffled feelings.

'I know just how you feel, darling. I'd like to bite someone tonight, too. We've both been badly used.'

The day had been too much for her, waiting for news of Regan, caring for Aaron and Hannah, the housework, then Jordan and that violent emotional scene. She needed a shower and a sleep, and she needed to cry, but she wouldn't do that until she had rung Drew. She dialled his number.

'Hello, Drew Hewitt here.'

At the sound of his firm masculine voice, Rowan felt her throat clog up with tears.

'Is that you, Rowan? Is everything okay? I've been waiting for you to ring.'

'Everything's okay,' Rowan said in a flat unemotional voice. 'Jordan . . . Your baby brother is over his emotional crisis.'

'What's with you, Rowan? You sound dreadful. I'm coming right down to see you.'

'*Oh, no, you're not!*' Rowan exploded. 'I've had enough of your family for one day. I'm going to bed and if you come here I'll set the dog on you. Come to think of it, I've had enough of you for a lifetime. I never want to see you or speak to you again as long as I live. Is that understood?'

'No, it's not understood. What the blazes are you talking about? Did Jordan hurt you?'

'No, Jordan didn't hurt me, but he could have. Did you think raping me would have been therapeutic for him or for me?'

'I don't believe he did that.'

'Quite correct, it didn't go that far, but it could have. You told me to tie Khan up and that's unforgivable. You didn't know what would happen, but you were prepared to take the risk, with *my* body. Goodbye, Drew Hewitt. Don't call me, and I won't call you.' She banged the phone down and, blinded by tears, headed for the bathroom.

She wept herself to sleep. Drew Hewitt was a *monster*. She had fallen in love with a man who had been prepared to sacrifice her to prove his trust in his brother. As Jordan had pointed out, where would she have been if his faith had been misplaced? There was no need to question his feelings for her. Zero, minus. No man who had any regard for a girl would have placed her in such a position. She hated Drew Hewitt and . . . and . . . she fell asleep.

The sun was high in the sky when she awoke next morning, and Khan sat watching her with a humorous, half anxious, half quizzical expression in his golden eyes.

Rowan rolled out of bed and stretched luxuriously before bending to pat him. 'Poor fellow, yesterday was really tough on you. Today I'll make it up to you: all day to ourselves, no kids, no chain, and no men. We'll spend the whole day on the beach, you and I together, we'll run and play and we'll swim and laze, and when we're hungry we'll search in the bush for the wild banana passion-fruit and live like kings.'

Khan cocked his head on one side, his ears pricked expectantly then, sensing her carefree mood, responded with excited barks and bounded towards her joyously. She wrestled and romped with him until, exhausted and laughing, she pushed him out the back door.

'Go and find yourself a cat to chase while I do the housework and ring my mother, then we'll be off.'

Quickly she dressed, in trim shorts and top, made her bed and tidied the house, abandoning the thought of dusting and vacuuming as she had hardly been long enough in the place to make a mess. Taking her coffee and toast to the front step she basked in the brilliance of the hot sunshine and jewel-bright perfection of the day, watching the wheeling gulls and the other water birds busy searching for food.

Why was she so happy? It was crazy! After the storm of weeping last night, she should have woken with a throbbing head and heavy eyes but, inexplicably, her mood was one of bubbling joy and soaring, delicious exhilaration. She tried to focus on Jordan's inexcusable behaviour and it seemed trifling, so she turned her mind to Drew, his perfidy, his treachery, his unlovingness—and even that failed to put a dent in her golden mood. Her dream was in

tatters, she'd told him she never wanted to speak to him or
see him again, and here she was grinning like a Cheshire
cat. She must be a very shallow person, no depth of
character.

Even that thought made her laugh as she returned to
the kitchen and placed the call to her mother. Cheerfully,
she told her mother that Regan knew she was adopted, so
there was nothing to block her making contact when
Regan returned.

'I'm thrilled for you, darling. Will you stay on there or
come home for a while?'

'I'll leave that open for a bit. You'll tell Dad?'

'Immediately. He'll be so pleased. He'll probably ring
you tonight, but don't hang up yet. What am I to tell
Greg? He haunts the place, and he says you haven't
answered his letter yet. I feel quite sorry for him. Do you
think you'll ever get back together again?'

'No, that's quite impossible. What I felt for him was not
love at all. I'm glad I found out before it was too late. Tell
him, I'm sorry but I won't be answering his letter, there
would be no point.'

There was a short silence at the other end, then her
mother said with a lilt of laughter in her voice, 'How
intriguing. Do you know how they train bank tellers to
pick out counterfeit notes, Rowan?'

'No, but I'm sure you're going to tell me.' There was
deep suspicion in Rowan's voice.

'They train them day after day counting the real stuff,
piles and piles of it, so that when they meet a fake, they
know instantly the false one, by its weight and texture. I
think it could be the same with love—only when you've
met the real thing can you recognise what is false.'

Rowan laughed. 'How very perceptive of you, Mother
darling, but I'm not prepared to satisfy your curiosity.
Goodbye now.'

Quickly she packed lunch for herself and Khan and

popped her bikini in the bag. The tide was out now, but she would lie in the sun and sand until it came in again. With Khan at her side she made her way down the hill. Was that why this festival feeling overflowed her whole being this morning? Because she was in love! She loved Drew Hewitt and it hardly mattered that this was a one-sided romance, and that it was going nowhere. Loving him seemed enough for this day. That's why she could not share it with her mother. There was nothing to share.

'We have the freedom of the city, Khan, so we'll march up the main street . . . no more hiding . . . from today the whole world can know I'm Regan's sister.'

Towards evening, after a wonderful day, Rowan climbed the hill with a sense of anticipation. When would she meet Drew again? Maybe, just maybe, he'd ring tonight. And if he did, and if he apologised, then she would be charmingly gracious and forgive him. After all, Jordan had said she was very like Regan in that she wouldn't bear a grudge. Surely Drew would know that also. Of course he would. He knew her better than Jordan did, he had spent more time with her.

When the phone rang after dinner she flew to answer it, breathless with excitement, but it was only her father, and the disappointment was devastating. She received her father's congratulations on her progress enthusiastically and, buoyed up by his encouragement, returned to the lounge somewhat restored. It was early yet, Drew was probably still out on the farm working. Farmers worked all hours while the fine weather held. He would ring as soon as he got in.

But he didn't ring. She got up and switched the TV off as transmission ended close to midnight, and as she prepared for bed, fear replaced the feeling of expectant joy. What if he never rang? What if he took her at her word and never spoke to her again? Perhaps he was pleased to have such an opportunity to break off the relationship, if she could describe such a short acquaintance that way. He had not really enjoyed being attracted to her, he had fought against it, and he had said he would never marry. What more likely than that he should grab at the first chance to finish seeing her?

She lay sleepless in her bed, agonising over her choice of words last night. She could have been more mature, instead of reacting so violently. She could have showed her outrage less dramatically. Pain at the thought of not seeing him again became a physical thing swallowing her up, and she turned over and buried her head in her pillow, and felt Khan move at her feet to accommodate her new position. Well, he wasn't going to get Khan back. She needed Khan.

What if she rang Drew up? What good would it do if he had made up his mind? She had had one sample of that treatment on the road the first Saturday she was in the Bay. She wouldn't leave herself open to that again. Why should he want her friendship? He had all he wanted . . . Rowan safely away on her art course, Jordan in the hills sorting out his problem. Drew didn't need her.

She rolled over again, disturbing Khan. Well, she needed Drew, most awfully she needed Drew. She wouldn't expect an apology . . . she would pretend there hadn't been anything to worry about if only he would ring. And if he didn't ring . . . Well, in a town this size, he couldn't avoid her forever. She was bound to meet him in the street and she would just walk up to him and start talking. It could happen tomorrow, in the morning. The ache in her heart started to ease. He had kissed her . . . and he had liked kissing her. It was hours before sleep came.

She didn't see Drew when she went into the town next day and the phone didn't ring . . . not once. The next day was the same and by evening she was feeling so low and dejected it was almost unbearable. He wasn't going to come back. She had just better face facts. What had

Jordan called loving Drew? An exercise in futility. She wouldn't stay in Collingwood, not month after empty month. She couldn't face that. Jordan could let her know when Regan returned.

The Mazda roared up the hill and reversed into the garage, and Khan stalked to the back door, his hair bristling, and he growled deep in his throat.

Rowan ran to the door. 'You *sit*, Khan. Jordan won't hurt me.' She opened the door. 'Come in, Jordan. Watch out for Khan.'

'Lock him in the bedroom.'

'No, I won't do that. You can both behave yourselves in a civilised manner, or I'll lock myself in the bedroom. *Sit*, Khan. You sit too, Jordan. Do you want coffee?'

'That would be nice,' Jordan said, taking a chair but keeping a wary eye on the immobile Khan, who was a frozen statue of displeasure.

Rowan boiled the kettle and brought the coffee to the table, pushing Jordan's mug across to him.

'Thanks, Rowan. What's been happening while I've been out of circulation? Don't tell me! Nothing. It's a dull town when I'm away.' His intelligent hazel eyes narrowed. 'You're looking a bit drawn. Has Drew been doing a bit of fine tuning on your emotions?'

'I haven't so much as set eyes on your brother since you left,' Rowan said sharply.

'Ah, that could account for it then. Do you miss having him about?'

'Not in the least,' Rowan flared at him.

Jordan grinned mischievously. 'And you were the girl lecturing me on honesty!'

Rowan felt a red tide sweep over her cheeks. 'Okay, I lied. I'm sorry. I do miss him, but I told him not to visit again, so I've got no complaints. Anyway, people who ask impertinent personal questions should expect evasive answers.'

'It was very pertinent as you'll see after I talk with you. I had a fantastic time up on Boulder Lake, not a soul for miles . . . just me and my conscience.'

'You shouldn't associate with such a dull companion,' Rowan replied, still smarting from being caught out in a lie. It was not her habit to lie, but to tell one to Jordan of all people made her furious with herself and with him.

Jordan's eyes lit with laughter. 'I love it when you're nasty to me. I should get used to it, but I can't. My conscience is no longer dull, I've got it back in working order. I'm a changed character, can't you see the improvement?'

'No, but then I haven't got a microscope.'

Jordan chuckled. 'Don't you want to hear my plans for the future?'

Rowan eyed him sternly. 'I haven't time to listen to fairy-tales.'

Jordan laughed again, and held his hand up in an exaggerated gesture. 'The truth, the whole truth, and nothing but the truth.'

'Okay. What are you going to do?' As she watched him she felt there was a change in him, something about his eyes, not so arrogant—confident perhaps, but not arrogant—and his teasing lacked malice.

'I'm going to marry Regan,' he stated flatly.

'If she'll have you.'

'Oh, ye of little faith, of course she'll have me. I'm a changed character. I told you so.'

'And I'm supposed to take your word for that . . . the evidence is too flimsy.'

'Right, I'll make you eat those cynical words, Rowan, and you'll be only one of many who'll write to Regan and tell her what wonderful husband material I am.'

'I might be prepared to do that if I was staying on, but as I won't see the miracle in action you'll have to pick on someone else,' Rowan objected.

'*You can't leave.* You said you were prepared to stay until Regan returned. You said it would take a lot of effort to change and for me to count the cost. Well, I've done that, and I'm prepared to give it a go, but only if you stay and cheer me on. I'll never make it on my own. I'll need support, I'll need encouragement, and lots and lots of praise. I'm counting on you, Rowan. You can't do this to me.' He leaned across the table and caught her hand. 'You'd be doing it for Regan, too, and I thought you wanted her to be happy.'

Rowan jerked her hand away, and bit her lip. She had certainly started something when she got stuck into Jordan the other night. Was it fair to walk out now? One look at him told her he was deadly serious; there was no laughter in his eyes, just an appeal that was hard to refuse. But it wasn't fair to her to ask her to stay when Drew had finished with her.

'You'd make it on your own. You've got enough determination,' she said, trying to believe it.

'No, I haven't.' He shrugged his shoulders and slumped back in the chair. 'If you're not prepared to help . . .'

'You're blackmailing me,' she spluttered angrily. 'It's your life, you fix it and let me get on with my own.'

He just sat there staring at her across the table, not saying a word, willing her to give in, his jaw stubbornly set.

'Okay, okay, but the change had better be fairly dramatic, fairly visible, and fairly fast. Don't think you can con me again, Jordan Hewitt. And I'm only doing this for Regan. I don't owe you or Drew any consideration. Not one *iota*.'

'I'd like to kiss you, Rowan,' he said softly as he sat up.

'Forget it. I'll hit you, Khan will bite you . . . need I go on?'

'No,' he was laughing. 'I did say I needed encouragement.'

'Not that much. Each time you've kissed me you've pretended I'm Regan. It's not much of a compliment.'

He sighed, 'No, I suppose it isn't. I'm sorry.' Then he smiled again. 'Except for the first time: that kiss wasn't for Regan.'

'You're *impossible*. Now tell me your plans.'

'Got any more coffee?'

'Yes, you carry on while I make it.' She needed more coffee herself. She felt she had made a stupid decision, but there was no turning back. Her father had said, 'Think positively, make the most of your opportunities,' and at least she would meet Regan without a sense of guilt if she gave Jordan all her support.

'Well, first thing is to get in old McKinnon's good books, and that's not going to be easy. But he offered me work on his farm while Regan's away and he hasn't rescinded that offer, so I'm going to take him up on it. He has had no reason to alter the terms . . .'

'How can you say *that*, Jordan?' Rowan cried indignantly as she handed him his coffee. 'It was because of your behaviour that he had to rush Regan away.'

'Not at all. I just met a pretty girl and asked her to the dance with me. Hardly a criminal action.'

'But your motives were certainly suspect.'

He smiled nonchalantly. 'Very hard things to prove, motives. Actually, I'm given a reputation for a lot of evil and devious schemes when I hardly deserve such credit. I'm a creature of impulse; when something strikes me as amusing I go ahead and do it. I saw you and I thought it would be hilarious to take you to the dance, and so it proved to be. All that rubbish about trying to get Regan pregnant, or trying to ruin her reputation, was all in Drew's mind. I'm not responsible for what people think, am I?'

'No . . . I suppose not,' Rowan agreed doubtfully.

Amusement sparkled in his bright eyes. 'Try believing

me. It will be easier all round. And I'll try and restrain my impulses.'

'Okay,' Rowan agreed, wondering if she was a complete imbecile, but it could be true.

'Tomorrow morning I'll present myself pure in thought, word and deed, willing in body and spirit, to work for McKinnon. He'll explode, but he's a man of his word and he'll take me on, then he'll try and work me to death. It will be a battle of the giants.'

'Is he really hard to get on with?' Rowan demanded anxiously.

'The worst. But I'm in good physical shape, so as long as I keep my head down and my lip buttoned, I should survive. Don't you admire my attitude?'

'Yes, I do, but can you sustain it?'

'Yes, I can. You see, up in the mountains I tried very hard to imagine what life would be like without Regan, and I couldn't. She is precious and dear, and without her my life wouldn't be worth living. So that really was the hardest decision to make, and it followed automatically that to win her I had to change. If there has to be a test then I welcome it. Whether it's to climb Mount Everest, become a Trappist monk for a time, or work for that old slave-driver McKinnon, I intend to win.'

'See, I told you that you didn't need me.'

'But I do. You will tell me if I'm missing the target, and I really couldn't take it from anyone else. That's why you're important. I can't explain why I let you bawl me out the other night, but I did let you, and I'll let you again, if necessary, but don't presume on it.'

'I won't,' Rowan said in a thoughtful tone. 'But what is the target? I have to know that. Isn't it just to gain Mr McKinnon's approval, hard though it might be? You'll know you're winning by his reaction.'

'No, it's more than that. Regan isn't conventional. She doesn't want me to prove I can hold down a steady job for six months, she doesn't care if I'm a beachcomber, and money doesn't mean a lot to her. She's a funny kid, all hooked in to law and order and respect for authority. I think the law is an ass and treat it accordingly. I use it, abuse it, test it, challenge it . . . well, it's just a laugh.'

She watched his green-hazel eyes brimming with mischief and knew he was reflecting on some of his escapades. 'And I'm supposed to turn you into a law-abiding citizen! No thanks, I know my limitations.'

'Relax, I'll do that bit myself. Regan says I'm like a matador flirting my cape at an enraged bull, and while I'm pretty nippy, someday I'll get gored. Then I'll either get sour and blame society for their stupid laws, or become more reckless, and what was a game will turn into a way of life. She's just not prepared to live that way, looking nervously over her shoulder every time she sees a policeman.'

'Smart girl, my sister Regan,' Rowan said.

'Oh, I'm not admitting she's right,' Jordan said with a provoking grin. 'But it's only a bit of fun, not important to me, and she is, *very* important.'

'So you've said,' Rowan smiled back at him. No wonder Regan found him hard to resist. The combination of his charm, his fantastic good looks, and his irrepressible sense of humour was enough to bewitch and bewilder any girl.

'You're smiling, what a break-through. I thought you'd forgotten how to . . . I shouldn't have left you all alone. Bet you haven't smiled since I went up the hills.'

Rowan looked away quickly so that he wouldn't see the pain in her eyes. The day he left she couldn't stop smiling, but now . . . 'You flatter yourself,' she said harshly.

'Only when no one else does,' he said nonchalantly. 'I can see you're waiting with bated breath for your part in this new scenario of mine.'

'Why not call it a miracle?' Rowan suggested sourly.

'If you like,' Jordan agreed cheerfully. 'Regan is always

praying that I'll change, and she believes that more things in heaven and earth are accomplished by prayer than this world dreams about, so we must give her a share of the credit.'

'She can have all my share,' Rowan said sarcastically.

'No, she can't, you've got a lot to do. First you've got to get Drew eating out of your hand, so that he'll . . .'

'Bite it off,' Rowan suggested grimly.

'I'm serious . . .'

'So am I,' Rowan said flatly. 'I'm not having anything to do with Drew Hewitt.'

'Oh, yes, you are. I need Regan's address so that I can write to her. If she doesn't know that I'm prepared to change my life around for her, she just may get interested in someone else. I'm not prepared to have that happen.'

'I could live with it,' Rowan told him firmly. 'Especially if it means . . .'

'Listen to me,' Jordan shouted. 'You need her address, too. Don't you want to write and tell her you're here on the spot? She knows she's adopted, sure, but she mightn't have heard she's got a twin sister. I think it's unfair that the whole district knows and she's the only one kept in the dark. She'll be thrilled out of her socks, and why deny her that pleasure? She could be away for six months or a year. Don't you want to write to her, get to know her a little before you meet? I'd have thought you would.'

'Of course I would,' Rowan said angrily. 'But why bring Drew into it?'

'Because it's necessary. I'll work on McKinnon, but it will take weeks and weeks. If Drew works on McKinnon it's a certainty that we'll be in touch with Regan by the end of the month. McKinnon thinks he's the greatest. He'll give him the address, and if you work on Drew he'll give it to you. A two-pronged attack, see. If I get it, I'll give it to you; if you get it, you give it to me. Agreed?'

'No, not agreed. I told Drew I didn't want to see him or

speak to him ever again. If you think I'm going to crawl back to him . . .'

'Of course not,' Jordan looked shocked at the thought. 'I wouldn't *expect* that of you. But, say Drew rang up and asked you for a date, could I count on you to put your pride aside and accept the invitation, just to help Regan and me? We'd be terribly grateful.'

Rowan wanted to refuse but was unable to deny the appeal in his eyes. 'Okay. In the unlikely event of Drew ringing me up and asking me out, I will accept, and I will ask him for Regan's address, but don't ask me to do anything else.'

'I have your word on that?' Jordan insisted.

'Yes, you have my word. Now go home, I'm tired.'

Jordan stood up, his face wreathed in smiles and amusement sparkled in his eyes. 'Drew will be in touch, that's a promise, but it may take a week or two.'

'You *haven't* changed, Jordan,' Rowan was furious. 'You've just manipulated me into an unenviable position and now you're going home to do the same to Drew.'

'Correct, but I haven't lied to you. Surely that's an improvement, you'll agree.'

'Out, get out! I don't know what Regan sees in you. You're outrageous!'

'Can I borrow your car?'

'No, no, you cannot. Find your own way home.'

'I won't be able to come and see you for a while if I haven't got a set of wheels.'

'I'll steel myself against such a crushing disappointment.' Rowan walked over and opened the door. 'Goodnight.'

'Goodnight. It's going to be fun having you for a sister-in-law. Such a gentle, loving nature you have.'

'It won't happen. You'll slip back into your old ways within a week,' Rowan jeered.

The laughter disappeared from his eyes. 'You're wrong.

This time I'm playing for keeps. Goodnight, my sweet.'

Rowan slammed the door behind him and locked it. He was a monster, too, just like his brother Drew. What had she let herself in for? Her mother used to warn her when she was little, 'If you play with the big boys you'll get hurt. They play too rough for you.'

Well, Jordan and Drew were big boys all right, and they played rough, but she had had her warning—and she had no intention of getting hurt.

CHAPTER SEVEN

ROWAN slept late and woke still feeling tired and definitely out of sorts in spite of the hours in bed. She pulled on her clothes and sneakers without enthusiasm.

'Come on, Khan, we'll go for a race along the beach, it might sort me out.'

Grumpily she stomped down the hill, irritated by Khan's eager anticipation and abundant energy. 'It's all right for you to be so cheerful, dog, your world hasn't fallen to pieces. Drew loves you. And why does he love you? Because of your almost reckless love and undivided loyalty. Yet when I'm prepared to offer him the same, it turns him off.'

As she started to run she pounded her feet savagely into the firm dry sand as if trying to drive away her ugly mood. She loved this long curving strip of beach, empty of people, beautiful beyond description: the native bush on one side, the flats and the shimmering waters on the other; the fresh clean invigorating air, and the bright and cloudless blue of the day. But there was no joy in her now.

As she turned for home she increased her pace and, as always, the smooth invigorating rhythm began to regenerate her flagging spirits. She flopped in the sand near the old wharf piles and, laughing a little breathlessly, pushed Khan away.

'Lean on yourself, Khan, I'm too tired to nurse you. I'm tired of your master Drew Hewitt, too. Life is for living, so I'm going to forget him. He hasn't been near me for days, so I won't get all bubbly and excited when Jordan makes him ring me.

'I'll be real cool! What girl would want a man who has

to be manipulated and cajoled into taking her out . . . not this girl. I'm like Regan, I want a *real* man, not someone hiding behind a mask, having to be prodded and prompted to get his act together. I want someone who knows what he wants and goes after it. That description doesn't fit Drew Hewitt.'

She sprang to her feet and marched to the road. She would ring Rochelle and take her and the children to Nelson for the day—that would take her mind off Drew. She wanted a young Lochinvar for her man, not a laggard in love and a dastard in war. She felt vital and vibrant and alive again.

Then, as she paused at the corner of the beach road by the attractive white bungalow, the heady heavy perfume of the massive datura tree laden with blossoms swamped her, and instantly in her thoughts she was back in Drew's arms, his lips on hers and the white blinding light seemed to enfold her in its warmth. She stopped, stricken for a moment, her face wet with tears, her composure demolished. That one man could make her feel love to such soul-shattering intensity when he was miles away, when she had known him such a short time, left her raw with pain.

Angrily she brushed her eyes, and hurried for home, quoting out loud almost in desperation!

'O, young Lochinvar is come out of the west;
Through all the wide Border his steed was the best.'

Safely inside, she moved to the phone to ring Rochelle but, even as she stretched out her hand, the machine rang stridently. Rowan reached to pick it up.

'Drew Hewitt here, Rowan. You must have been waiting for my call. That's nice.'

His voice melted her bones. Cool, remember, *cool*. 'Not really, I was just going to ring Rochelle.'

'I'm glad you're back. It seems ages since I saw you. Did you enjoy yourself?'

Rowan blinked with surprise. 'Enjoy myself, where?' She was proud of her casual tone.

'Up in the mountains with Jordan. Boulder Lake is remarkably lovely. You must have been fit to make it.'

Rowan took the phone from her ear and stared at it in shock. What *was* he talking about? 'Who told you I was in the hills with Jordan?' she managed with magnificent calm. 'Did Jordan tell you?'

'No, I haven't spoken to Jordan yet. I saw him over with McKinnon earlier when I was mustering the cattle. As soon as I saw him I knew you'd be home, so galloped in to give you a buzz. I've missed you, Rowan.'

'It's always nice to be missed,' she replied in a husky voice, fighting the tears that threatened. He wasn't ringing because Jordan had been working on him—he hadn't even spoken to Jordan. And he had missed her. She thought her heart would burst with joy.

'Haven't you missed me?' There was a lilt of laughter in his tone.

She imagined his eyes crinkling with that incredible smile. 'Just a little, but you still haven't told me where you got your news from.'

'Oh, Jordan's mother thought she saw you on the road to Bainham. Well, I knew it was you, but she thought it was Regan. She's a bit behind with the gossip, having been away. She only told me to try and shatter me, knowing how I protect Regan.'

'And did it shatter you?' she asked lightly.

'More than somewhat. I know I told you to help him, but I did say there were limits. Actually, I thought she was mistaken, so in the morning I leapt into my station-wagon and zoomed down to check and there was no sign of you or Khan, so I had to believe her. I rang on the hour every hour all day, but getting no reply I gave up about five.'

Rowan's mind was whirling. He had driven right down that first morning while she had been so blithely happy wandering on the beach, knee-deep in love with him. And he had rung all day, only giving up about the time she returned. 'I didn't go with Jordan. I've been here all the time.'

He swore, then swiftly apologised. 'Oh, Rowan, look at all that wasted time. Why didn't you ring me?'

'There were reasons,' she said flatly.

'Let's not go into that. Will you invite me to lunch today? I'd like to see you.'

'Not today. Sorry, Drew, but I'm going to Nelson. I hope to take Rochelle and the kids with me.' Caution had taken over her reeling senses. He might have missed her, he might want to see her, but he was still not a marrying man. The raw pain that overwhelmed her by the datura tree was too recent to forget.

'Blast! I've got cattle to load and then I'm leaving for a business trip to Southland, and I'll be gone ten days. I'm buying some stags and have several deer farms to visit. Come with me, Rowan.'

Temptation swept over her like a flood-tide; to travel with him, to be with him days and nights, both in a holiday mood . . . That one word holiday stopped her cold in her tracks. She did not want a brief interlude of happiness with Drew, it had to be a life-time or nothing. From somewhere she mustered the strength to say, 'Not likely. I've got work to do if you haven't. I might be taking care of Rochelle's children if she goes back nursing. She could even start this week.'

He laughed. 'It was worth a try. Still, I'll console myself that you'll be staying a while in the Bay. Say, I've got tickets for a play in Nelson Friday week. Will you go with me? It should be good, it was a sell-out in London and in Australia, and we could have dinner together first.'

'I'd love to.'

'Great. Have you seen Jordan yet?'

'Yes, he was here last night. He's okay.'

'I know I can thank you for that, but be careful. Don't tie Khan up while I'm away.'

'That's a promise,' Rowan said with a happy laugh.

'Great. I wish I could see you before I go. I wish I could kiss you goodbye. Won't you put your trip off until tomorrow?'

Her palm felt slippery with perspiration as she fought the desire in her heart to be with him. 'No, Drew.'

'You're a hard girl, Rowan, hard-hearted. Oh, I meant to tell you Regan rang me from Auckland before she left, and I told her all about you. She was so excited, nearly changed her mind about going, and you know how much that meant to her. She made me promise to keep you in the Bay whatever it took, until she got back. I'll give you her address when I return as long as you don't give it to Jordan.'

Rowan bit her lip until she tasted blood. So this was what all this sweet-talk was! 'Whatever it took'. He was still trying to fix the world for his little mate, Regan. Thank God she hadn't said she would travel South with him.

'Are you still there, Rowan?' he asked sharply. 'I thought you'd be pleased.'

'Ecstatic,' she forced herself to say. 'But why can't Jordan have the address? It really means a lot to him.'

'He can't have it because I say so. He'd not be content to write, he'd go rushing off after her.'

'Who do you think you are? *God?* Making decisions in people's lives like that, Drew Hewitt! Goodbye.' She slammed the receiver down and burst into tears. How dare he just use her like that! Well, she would use him until she got that address and then she would give it to Jordan. She rushed out of the house with Khan at her heels and ran up the hill to Rochelle's.

As she saw them on the front lawn she called, 'Do you lot want a trip to Nelson today? It's my shout, lunch and all the trimmings. Do say you'll come. I need conpany today.'

'Try and stop us,' Rochelle scrambled to her feet, brushing her bright hair away from her face. 'We'll be ready in ten minutes. You're an angel.'

Rowan waved and turned back down the track. 'I'm going to tie you up, Khan. I'm sorry, but you wouldn't enjoy sharing with Aaron and Hannah all day. I'll make it up to you tomorrow. Oh, Khan, don't look at me like that. I *need* somebody to keep loving me.'

She clipped the chain on and then bent and hugged him, her tears cascading down her cheeks and falling like diamonds on his sleek coat. He frantically tried to cheer her, licking her face, tugging at her sleeve, whimpering anxiously in sympathy.

'Sorry, love, I shouldn't upset you.' She knuckled her eyes and forced a smile as she patted him affectionately before going into the house to shower and change.

The day went amazingly well and they enjoyed the trip enormously, buying lunch to eat at Tahunanui Beach. Rowan and Rochelle sat in the sun watching the children crawl through the tunnels, climb on the tortoises, swing on the swings and turn the roundabouts.

'You're looking happier now, Rowan. What on earth happened this morning? You looked like a dam about to burst, all heaped up with tension and strain.'

Rowan glanced at her sideways. 'Thanks for not asking before now, I couldn't have found the words to describe my mood. It's Drew Hewitt. I don't know what it is about him, but he either makes me feel deliriously happy or in the depths of despair. I really am not a moody person; until I came here I was reasonably serene and tranquil, but I can zip from the sublime to the gorblimey in seconds, from radiating bliss to utter blah.'

Rochelle slanted her a teasing glance. 'Could be love. Sounds like love.'

'How would I know? Two months ago I was all set to waltz up to the altar with Greg. Makes me shudder to think of how close I got to being tied to him for life.'

'Does Jordan have the same effect on you?' Rochelle asked.

'Hardly.' Rowan smiled. 'Jordan is a fascinating character, superbly handsome, wickedly amusing, and always exasperating, but if I never saw him again it would almost be a relief. But Drew, he dominates all my waking moments and most of my sleeping ones. To meet him, even to talk to him on the phone, makes me feel like a hang-glider or an eagle caught in an updraught, soaring upwards effortlessly, leaving the earth behind. It's breathtaking, dangerous, exciting and exhilarating, then . . . then "cwash down".'

'What do you mean?'

'Oh, he says something that shows me he only takes me around to keep tabs on me for Regan, and I plummet downwards. There's a bird somewhere, called the Gooney bird, I think, and it never can land gracefully, just bumps along tumbling over and over, an awkward mass of flesh and feathers. In the sky it's magnificent, on earth it's a mess. That's me.'

Rochelle laughed. 'That's some simile, I can't imagine you anything but graceful. But you mean if you knew that Drew felt the same way about you, you'd never have to come down to earth.'

Rowan shrugged her shoulders. 'Probably, but would it last? How do you know love from infatuation?'

'If you have to ask, it's infatuation.'

'You'd be an authority,' Rowan snapped without thinking. 'Oh, I'm sorry, Rochelle, I didn't mean to hurt you.'

'You didn't.' Rochelle pulled a face. 'Just because Jim and I mucked up our chance, doesn't mean I didn't pick the right man. He was the same, he knew. He came into a party where I was and he looked across at me, and he called it spontaneous combustion. He took me home and we barely spoke a dozen words. It was so strange. Then he came back next night and asked me to marry him.'

'And you felt the same way?'

'Yes.' Her bright eyes were shining. 'When he came into a room everyone else blurred as if they were out of focus, and only he was real.'

'But it didn't last,' Rowan said sadly.

'Who said it didn't last?' Rochelle replied roughly, getting to her feet. 'I feel the same way about Jim today as I did the night I met him, and I probably will till the day I die. So if what you feel for Drew is the real thing, grab him, and hold him, and never let anything come between you, not mortgages and in-laws, nor kids and wet naps, not even tiredness, and old girl-friends. If someone had given me this advice earlier, I'd have something warmer to cuddle up to in bed than my beastly pride.'

Rowan walked beside her towards the children. 'Why don't you try and get together again, if you love him . . . ?'

Rochelle laughed without mirth. 'You and Regan, you are a pair. She's praying it will all come right, and she believes in miracles. Me, I don't. Jim has his pride, I have mine and never the twain shall meet.'

Rowan scooped Hannah, protesting vigorously, into her arms. 'I wouldn't discount Regan's prayers, not after seeing the change in Jordan. Now, Hannah, what col-oured ice-block do you want?'

'Gween!' Hannah's enormous blue eyes fastened on Rowan's intently, then she beamed rapturously. 'Nee, too.'

'Yes,' Rowan chuckled. 'Aaron, too. What colour for you, Aaron?'

'Red.' He ran to take her outstretched hand.

'You'd buy my kids' affection with ice-blocks?' Rochelle protested, as she gathered up jerseys and sandals.

'Of course. And I'd buy happiness for you and for me,

too, if it only cost twenty cents and was easily available at the corner store.'

'Try prayer,' Rochelle scoffed. 'It's cheaper.'

'I might do just that,' Rowan replied thoughtfully and saw in Rochelle's eyes a flicker of hope break through the bright cynicism for a brief second.

Driving home, Rowan viewed the next ten days with an incredible lack of enthusiasm. Was she going to be like Rochelle, loving a man but not living with him? Even if Drew was in love with her, he would never admit it, because to do so meant he would have to take her to live with Jordan and his mother, or agree to sell Bonnie Doon. He would never do that—Jordan said Drew would rather be dead than leave the farm. Oh, it was impossible.

Yet somehow the days passed, and some she even enjoyed. Sunday she spent out at Westhaven with Jordan and Khan. The second week Rochelle started at the hospital, job-sharing with a farmer's wife who was also an ex-nurse, and Rowan really enjoyed caring for the children every second day.

After the children went home on Friday afternoon, Rowan washed her hair and prepared her mind to meet Drew. She had decided to be even more careful than before, if necessary to pretend to have a vital interest in Jordan. Anything was better than Drew finding out she loved him and having him resort to his well-practised ruses to detach himself from unwanted females.

She chose a simple sand-coloured sleeveless dress with a tiny silver thread that shone as she moved, like the sun on the glittering sands. Her hair was shining and loose on her shoulders and her eyes more vividly blue than she could ever remember. With her even tan, and heightened colour in her cheeks, she needed a minimum of make-up, and on her final check in the mirror she knew she had never looked lovelier.

She sat on the verandah step, her long slender silk-clad legs and elegant strap sandals thrust out before her as if to brace herself against Drew's coming. Her father said she had hidden talents; well, acting wasn't one of them. As she heard Khan yelping with excitement as he raced to greet Drew, she knew that her own blatant eagerness to see him was equally obvious.

And then he was there, tall, tanned, lithe and powerful, and in his grey eyes the same smiling delight she was experiencing, and she could hardly breathe. She was soaring on the upthrust of a mighty wind . . .

He caught her slim hands in a bone-crushing grip. 'Have I missed you! It seems like a year. Let's cancel this dinner and play, and just sit and talk and watch the sun go down together.'

Wordlessly she shook her head. She wasn't that strong, she needed people around her, words, music and food, anything to keep up the fragile barrier against her own weakness.

'Okay. I'm sorry I'm a bit late. I'll tie Khan while you go out to the car.'

She walked out to the road-side on wobbly legs. She had to keep him at a distance. She had to pretend that this was just a pleasant interlude in her life, that she didn't expect this attraction to last, that she was modern and broad-minded, and not interested in marriage—in fact, definitely against it. She would talk to him about Jordan, about Jordan's suggestion that she should come and work for Mr McKinnon two or three days a week. That would annoy him, and she wouldn't be able to explain why she had even considered such a crazy offer.

But she didn't tell him. She sat by his side all the way to Nelson just revelling in his company, laughing with him, talking with him, and loving him with her mind. Again and again Rochelle's words kept returning, 'If it's real, grab him and hold him, and let nothing ever separate you.' Great advice to give a girl in love with a confirmed bachelor.

The meal and the wine were superb, the play hilarious yet vastly entertaining and, as always, time spent with him rushed by on wings, completely opposite to the way it dragged achingly along when they were apart.

On the way home she broached Jordan's proposition. 'I'm thinking of going to work for Mr McKinnon. Jordan said that he's really going downhill since Regan left, doesn't make the effort to feed himself or bother at all. He just eats bread and cheese for breakfast, lunch and dinner.'

'And you feel sorry for him?' Drew demanded sharply.

'Not exactly.'

'Then what *exactly* do you hope to achieve? If it's Jordan's idea, you'd better examine it pretty closely. He doesn't do anything without an ulterior motive.'

'Could be me that has the ulterior motive. Did you consider that?' Rowan said aggressively.

'You're not going to do it.' Drew made it a flat statement.

'Oh, yes, I am.' Rowan had only been toying with the idea; now, because of his opposition, she decided to accept.

'Jordan may think it's a terrific idea, but McKinnon wouldn't have you in the house.'

'He told Jordan to bring me up to meet him,' she flung at him.

'I won't let you go there. Look, you've never been inside the place—it's primitive. He wouldn't let his wife or Regan spend a penny on it. Regan didn't worry much, not being housekeeping-minded—all her spare time she spent painting. You cried when you saw the outside—you'll pass out when you see the inside.'

They drove on in angry silence the rest of the way over

the mountain. Rowan was filled with conflicting emotions; unhappy because the evening that had been such fun was ending so dismally; relieved in a way that the quarrel was covering up her real feelings from him; and worried about the McKinnon job.

As they reached the Waiapu Bridge, Drew swung the car sharply left off the main road and Rowan realised that they were heading towards the Pupu Springs. She sat stiffly in her seat, wondering what was in his mind.

'Come along, Rowan, we'll try and talk this out.' He opened the car door for her.

She walked silently beside him along the wooded path, marvelling at the exquisite beauty of the place, more lovely and mysterious in the silver moonlight than it had been in the bright sunlight. Her anger drained swiftly away and in its place came a longing to know if he cared for her at all. Was his feeling for her just like Jordan's, was he just using her as a substitute for Regan? For the first time she realised that being an identical twin wasn't all roses.

'Are you cold, Rowan?' His arm came around her as she leaned over the protecting rail and stared down into the dark green depths.

'No,' she replied breathlessly, her heart pounding at his closeness, and the intensity of her love for him. She wanted to turn and fling herself into his arms and beg him to love her, but it would be a futile exercise, as Jordan had said.

'Good. I want you to be comfortable while we talk. Tell me why you feel you must go to the McKinnon place?'

Comfortable didn't describe the way she was feeling as he gently massaged her bare arm, nor was she cold. She swallowed with difficulty. 'I've never hated anyone in my life, and the feeling I have for Mr McKinnon is the nearest thing to it I've ever experienced. I know it's ridiculous.

but every time I think of him looking down on those two helpless babies and choosing Regan and rejecting me, I am consumed with rage. I want to know what was wrong with me . . . why he didn't take us both. Quite frankly, I don't want to go near him, I don't even want to see what he looks like, or speak to him. And when Jordan talked him into getting a woman to clean the place a couple of times a week and offered me the job, I just laughed at him.'

'That's what you should have done. It's a ridiculous suggestion,' Drew said grimly.

'But it's not,' Rowan twisted around to face him, protesting. 'I have to face up to the fact he didn't want me, or his wife didn't, whichever. I suppose I should feel my birth-mother rejected me, but I don't, she tried to keep us together. If I work for him, I'll find some way of getting it out of him. He must have had a reason . . . to separate us like that. I want to know what it was. I have a *right* to know. My parents wanted us both, most people would. Why didn't he?'

'I wish you wouldn't, Rowan. You may get hurt worse than you are now. He's a pretty hard customer. I don't see him giving away any secrets.' Drew brushed her hair back from her face. 'You didn't do so badly out of the arrangement.'

'You don't have to tell me how lucky I am,' Rowan said angrily. 'But this is something I want to know and I'm going to find out. Why are you trying to stop me?'

He smiled down at her. 'My motives are not nearly as clear-cut as yours, Rowan. I'm deeply suspicious of Jordan and more so of old McKinnon. He's a very shrewd customer, old Mac. He doesn't want Jordan as a son-in-law, and is probably thinking along the lines that, if he has you both working for him, he can encourage Jordan to believe that you are more suited to his taste than Regan is.'

'And that wouldn't please you?' Rowan prompted against her better judgment, her eyes very blue and very innocent.

'No. It would not please me.' He pulled her closer and his lips came down on hers, demanding and possessive, and again the light was all about her, surrounding her, within and without.

As he lifted his head she stared at him, willing him to declare himself in words as well as in action. When he didn't speak, she said tauntingly, 'Jordan has already asked me to marry him.'

Drew looked down, relaxing his hold slightly. 'Jordan was always impulsive.'

'And you're not.'

'No, I'm not.' Drew watched her with a curious gleam in his eyes. 'You know the story about the hare and the tortoise, and you know who won.'

Rowan giggled. A tiny bubble of joy exploded somewhere inside her and filled her with a delicious sense of anticipation. Drew was looking at her with the same careful, measured scrutiny that her father so often bent on her, especially if he was planning something to surprise her with . . . and she knew also from long experience that to prod and pry would gain her nothing. Something wonderful was going to happen, not tonight, maybe not tomorrow, but before long . . .

'You find me amusing?' Drew demanded with mock severity.

'Hilarious.' She laughed out loud, her eyes sparkling. He would probably be annoyed to know he reminded her of her father, but to her it was a wonderfully endearing discovery. He had spoken of winning against Jordan. Winning what? Her love? Or Regan's?

He kissed her again and again, and the delight grew not less but more fantastic, as his body moulded against hers and their desire kindled like fire.

'I think I'd better take you home, Rowan,' he said abruptly.

'Yes, I think you should,' Rowan agreed. Yet she turned from him to stare down at the silent bubbling waters. So much she didn't understand, and she longed to know every little detail of his life. She could feel the power and the strength of his personality. There was honesty and determination and purpose in the way he spoke, the way he moved, yet he gave very little of his thoughts away. What had made her fall headlong in love with him? It wasn't only his looks and charm, although they couldn't be discounted. Did any woman ever know what basic ingredient drew her to one man above all others?

'What's worrying you, Rowan?' he asked gently.

'Nothing. I know so little about you; I was just wondering, that's all. How old were you when your mother died?'

He eyed her speculatively, as if trying to find the direction of her thinking. 'I was almost five, just started school. We survived some time with housekeepers then Dad remarried.'

'And didn't your stepmother ever like you?'

He laughed shortly. 'Oh, yes, she made a great fuss over me. I distinctly remember Dad asking if I'd mind her joining the family, and I reckoned it would be great. She changed after Jordan arrived, and life got a bit rough.'

'But didn't your father stand up for you?'

'He did his best, but she was his wife and Jordan his son, and he loved them, too. I spent a lot of time at the McKinnons', it became a second home, you know—after school, holidays. Then I was out on the farm with my father as much as possible. That was a bonus. I sort of absorbed farming knowledge, and it helped a lot when I had to take over here.'

'Was it hard to come back?'

'That's an understatement.'

'Was she jealous of you?'

'Could have been. I only know that she played each member of the family against the rest. It became impossible . . . well, it always had been. That's why I got bunged off to boarding school early, then to Telford, then to my mother's brother up North. I worked on his station until six years ago.'

Rowan wondered at the lack of bitterness in Drew. He was hard, strong, yet so casual. If he had lived with it all his life, she supposed he had got used to it. 'Yet you really like Jordan, don't you?'

'Oh, Jordan's okay. He's had a tougher row to hoe than me.'

'How?' Rowan stared at him incredulously.

'Well, think about it. She's his mother. Now, me, I have a picture of mine—loving, kind, sweet, perfect. She probably had faults, but I didn't know of them. But, Jordan loves his mother and has to watch her being spiteful, vindictive, manipulative, and he's not dumb. Then losing his father just when he needed him most, with me coming back in to take over, and his mother treating me as Big Brother, the Enemy. No wonder he's got a warped sense of humour.'

'And where does Regan fit into all this?'

He smiled. 'Oh, Regan. She's always been there. I told you I spent all my spare time there when she was little. She was a cute kid. When I came home I sort of fell into the habit of dropping in over there to get a bit of peace. She was only a schoolgirl, but her friendship meant a whole lot to me. When her mother died, she needed someone to lean on. We go back a long way, Regan and I.'

Rowan stared at the water. So he loved Regan, she could hear it in his voice. And Regan was in love with Jordan. Imagine choosing Jordan above *Drew*! Or had she? There was only Jordan's word for that, and Regan had rung Drew before leaving. Suddenly she found herself praying silently, God, don't let me be just a consolation prize because he can't have Regan. I couldn't bear that.

'Let's go home.' She turned wearily away. She was a Gooney bird again, not flying and soaring majestically above the earth, but just an awkward mass of tumbling feathers, crash landing. She walked down the steps. 'You said to me you had more patience than Jordan and his mother; does that mean if you wait long enough, someday you'll get the Bonnie Doon?'

Drew slipped his arm about her and walked in step along the wooded, moonlit path. 'Did you know patience is a gift? Regan said it was. I always thought of it as a negative quality until she explained it to me. That's Regan's way—she sees people through different eyes from the rest of us, and has the ability to make you feel good about yourself.'

'That's nice,' Rowan said, and waited for him to continue. When he didn't she felt it better not to prompt him. She was learning to know him a little better. He would open up when he was ready and not before, and it was good walking in companionable silence.

As they drove off he again picked up the thread of their discussion. 'Bonnie Doon . . . you know it's always been the most important thing in my life, I've aimed everything at loving it, working it, and believing that someday it would be mine, or belonging to Jordan and me in partnership. But just lately I've been wondering if it hasn't taken too many years of my life already. I do have other needs . . .'

'And what have you decided?' Rowan held her breath. Did he mean since she had arrived, or since Regan had gone away?

'That Jordan has had enough leeway. He's twenty-three now, the same age I was when I had to come back here. He's old enough to make a decision on the future. I don't want to decide his life-style, but conversely I have no intention of his choosing mine.'

Rowan let her breath out slowly. It wasn't anything to do with her or Regan, just Jordan. Another crash landing. 'Could you really face losing the Bonnie Doon?'

He flicked a glance at her with a grin. 'Oh, there'd be compensations . . . big ones.'

Again she was soaring on an upthrust of wind. If only he meant what she thought he meant. He might have the gift of patience, but she didn't. She wanted to know right now what he was thinking. 'When will you know?'

'At the end of this month. We have a meeting once a year with the solicitor and accountant to work out the programme for the coming year. I'm going to make my move then, and Jordan will have to decide whether to come in with me and buy his mother out, or I'll buy both of them out, and if there's no agreement on that, I'll vote with his mother to sell it.'

'You'd leave Collingwood?'

'No way. I belong here. There's a block of land down Westhaven I've been looking at. Regan's favourite saying is "If one door closes another one opens", and I've decided that I've been patient long enough, so if this door doesn't open, I'm going to put my shoulder to it and help it along.'

When they got home Drew let Khan go, then stood at the door looking down at Rowan. 'Can I see you tomorrow?'

'No. I've got a bit of sorting out to do for myself. I'll write to Regan and give it to you on Monday when I go to see Mr McKinnon.'

'So, you're still determined to work there.'

'I am.'

'Well, come in our drive, it's a shorter route, and that way I'll see you each morning and evening you're there. Also, I'll take you over and introduce you to McKinnon, that way he'll know you're my friend as well as Jordan's and he'll be a little more careful in his treatment of you.'

His kiss was long and satisfying and then he held her close, looking deep into her eyes. 'Take care, Rowan, I don't want you hurt.'

Through a blur of tears she saw him stride out to his car. How dumb he was! Daniel McKinnon couldn't hurt her. Only Drew Hewitt himself had that power. If he didn't want her, then she didn't care how may doors opened, because none of them would have any meaning.

CHAPTER EIGHT

ON Monday morning she drove towards Bonnie Doon with her emotions in a turmoil, in spite of the glorious golden day. She was fighting her nervousness at meeting Daniel McKinnon one minute, and trying to tone down her antagonism towards him the next. On the seat lay her letter to Regan, sealed and waiting for Drew to address it. Enclosed in it, also, was a letter from Jordan. In handing it over he had savagely attacked her for being an incompetent accomplice in not obtaining Regan's whereabouts. He had only calmed down when she threatened not to include his note at all, then, typically Jordan, he had become arrogantly confident Regan would ring him immediately after receiving his letter.

She sighed. She was irritated by his indestructible self-assurance, but wished she had more of it herself. Suddenly, she recalled the dream that had disturbed her sleep last night, so vivid that she had woken and it had taken ages to get back to sleep. Her lips curved into a smile. In the dream, a horseman had come riding at the gallop towards a girl dressed in a long, white, flowing wedding gown; his flamboyant and daring skill, and his plunging horse, made the girl's face glow with admiration at his impetuous arrogant style, and his astonishingly handsome face—young Lochinvar without doubt. Then she saw the rider was Jordan, and the girl herself . . . or Regan. Even as she watched, the girl waved him away and turned to walk up a hill with hands outstretched towards a man clad in shining armour, his face alight with love and his sword drawn in readiness to protect her . . . and the man was Drew.

For hours she had tried to work out what it meant, but could only decide that she no longer wanted an impulsive proud young Lochinvar, but would prefer any day a knight in shining armour, patient and protective, strong, yet so gentle. Perhaps the girl in the dream had been Regan, and it was just a warning that Regan also would choose Drew above Jordan. What a muddle it all was. Perhaps when Regan wrote back she would be straightforward about her feelings towards the brothers, but why should she? Rowan herself had been honest about everything except that particular point. It would be wonderful to hear from her twin after searching for months, even though the excitement might now be tinged with pain if she lost Drew.

As she parked by the boundary gate, Drew came striding from the house. 'Early on the job, aren't you?' He welcomed her with a smile.

Rowan smiled back, 'Thought I might cook him a good breakfast to start off on the right foot . . . that's if he takes me on. Here's my letter.'

He pocketed it. 'I'll put it in the mail this morning. Come on then, let's get it over. If he sends you away, you can spend the day mustering with me.'

It was a temptation to cancel the whole idea, but she braced her slim shoulders and picked up her basket and headed for the gate. 'Golly, this place has been tidied up.'

'That's Jordan, he's certainly bent on pleasing old Mac. He moved all the long grass and cleaned up the yard after he finished work on Saturday. It surely makes a difference. Oh, there's McKinnon now.'

Rowan looked up to see a long, lean man with grey hair and an Abe Lincoln face bearing down on her. She stopped apprehensively, wondering if it had been wise to wear the identical sundress that Regan had bought.

'Good-day, Mac, this is Rowan Chapman, a friend of

mine. Jordan told her you were needing some help in the house.'

McKinnon stared at her, without a flicker of expression in his pale blue Celtic eyes. 'We'll be into breakfast in half an hour.' He turned and walked back the way he had come.

'Is that it?' she gasped, looking at Drew.

Drew grinned. 'He's a man of very few words, when it suits him. Still, you must have given him quite a turn.'

'Well, I'd better go and make a start.'

'Would you like me to go in with you . . .'

'No thanks,' Rowan said firmly. 'You can take Khan with you for the day. He'll enjoy that better than being cooped up inside with me.'

She marched towards the cottage door without looking back at Drew; that way he wouldn't see how scared she was. She thrust open the door, and stepped inside. What an appalling mess! It was dark and gloomy, dusty and untidy, the linoleum worn and in some spots non-existent, the curtains faded and threadbare, the sink and table covered with dirty dishes and pots and pans. He couldn't have washed anything since Regan left. There wasn't a clear inch of space on the mantelpiece, sideboard, or sofa. There was total chaos everywhere she looked. Clothes and papers, tins and bottles, jostled for place among nuts and bolts and pieces of farm machinery. It was incredible.

But the coal fire was burning brightly, so there would be hot water and she would have their meal ready on clean plates when they came in, if it killed her. For the very first time she felt that she could equal Regan at something. She didn't mind housework, and creating order in this place would be the challenge of a lifetime. She found a pan, scrubbed it, and placed it on the range, then filled the kettle, glad that she had brought some groceries with her. She found an empty cardboard carton and removed everything off the table into it, except the dishes which she stacked on the floor near the sink, before scrubbing the table. Now she had some working space.

Jordan arrived first and, giving her a quick hug, said with a flashing smile, 'The bacon and eggs smell fantastic. I usually eat at home, but with you here, there is no contest. What a miracle—even a table-cloth!'

Warmed by his praise, Rowan replied, 'Just a clean tea-towel that I had in my basket. Jordan, is it always like this?' She waved her hand about the room.

'Almost. Regan just doesn't see it. She's out of doors most of the time, working for her father or painting. She eats here, sleeps here, and now and again tries to clean it up, but it was pretty hopeless. He gave her a mere pittance and that she spent on paints and the odd dress. Still, she was happy here with him . . .'

Daniel MacKinnon came in and silently took his place at the table. Rowan quickly served them with breakfast and made a hot cup of tea. When she placed his cup beside him he remarked, 'I like porridge for breakfast.'

Rowan's eyes flashed. There he was, eating the first decent meal he had had in weeks, obviously enjoying the fresh bread and butter, bacon and eggs that she had provided and he was growling. 'You'll get porridge Wednesday if you give me money for groceries, and if I can find a clean pot.'

Jordan winked at her, but she flounced back to the sink and started on her mammoth task. Who did he think he was, the ungrateful brute? Simmering with rage, she heard him and Jordan arguing about farm procedures and was glad that Jordan was winning hands down.

Daniel McKinnon carefully put a few dollars on the table before he left. 'Is that enough?'

'No, nothing like it. How long since you've been to the store? I want at least forty dollars, there's nothing in the cupboards.' She wasn't going to let him bully her.

Without speaking, he added the extra money and left.

All day she cleaned and scrubbed and tidied and went home completely exhausted, as much from the burning resentment as the actual physical exertion. The craggy old man refused even to speak to her unless absolutely necessary. Not a word of thanks for her efforts.

Tuesday was a delightful day, spent watching over Aaron and Hannah, and their laughter and exuberance quite restored her normal good humour.

Armed with a packet of washing powder as well as other necessities, she drove towards the farm next morning. She also had a casserole prepared so that she could spend the morning washing the mountain of clothes she had gathered up.

The day began disastrously and got worse. She let the porridge catch and she burnt the toast, because the toaster refused to pop. Then scalded her hand making the tea, having forgotten the loose nut on the kettle handle. The washing took four hours because she had to watch every article through the wringer as it had a malevolent habit of wrapping the clothes about its worn rollers and jamming, and then the clothes-line snapped with the load and she had to rinse and wring the whole wash again.

Daniel McKinnon did not speak to her at breakfast, and his only comment at lunch was that he preferred his main meal at midday. Rowan hoped he would choke on the cold meat and salad that he was eating with evident enjoyment. Not even Jordan's most valiant attempts to lift the mood at the table made her smile. She spent the afternoon vacuuming the rest of the house with a decrepit machine which drove her insane. If she jerked it forward the hose came out or the cord pulled free, so most of her time was spent replacing one or the other.

She had Daniel McKinnon's dinner ready after milking and surveyed her work with a jaundiced eye. The house was clean and dust-free, but not attractive. Nothing could make it that, with its faded and peeling dingy woodwork and wallpaper, and worn and tatty carpets and linoleum. No wonder Regan had not bothered. It was an abomination.

McKinnon cleaned himself up and settled down complacently at the table, waiting to be served. She slammed his meal down in front of him without a word. She knew Jordan wouldn't be in, so there was nothing to ease the tension between them. They both devoted themselves to their meals and Rowan was so angry and irritated by his stubborn silence that her food nearly choked her.

'You've been working very hard,' Daniel McKinnon said softly, looking at her with a blue piercing gaze.

'Yes,' Rowan replied, taken completely by surprise at his sudden attempt at conversation.

'What are you trying to prove?'

'Prove?' Rowan echoed blankly, staring at him.

'Yes, what are you trying to prove?' he repeated slowly, watching her with an unnerving scrutiny. 'That you are a good housekeeper? Are you trying perhaps to show up my girl in front of her father and friends? Is that it?'

That did it. Rowan pushed back her chair violently, and stood up, her hands on her slim hips. 'You wretched, ungrateful man. I came here and cooked for you and cleaned for you and not one word of thanks have you given me. All you can do is complain and criticise, and now you have the unmitigated gall to suggest I'm doing it to show Regan in a bad light. How could I show Regan up? You're the one who's being shown up. How could you keep her in such a hovel? She deserves better than this . . . any woman does. You keep your animals in more attractive surroundings. Why not splash a bit of paint around this place and have a stainless steel sink here? You ought to be ashamed of yourself. I know you've got no money . . .'

McKinnon stood up, towering over her. 'Who says I've got no money?'

'Everybody. But even if you're poor you could spend a

few dollars on wallpaper, paint and floor coverings. I wouldn't keep a dog in such drab and dismal conditions. And I hope when Regan sees how other people like that she'll be as disgusted as I am.'

'You have been misinformed. I am not a poor man. If I gave you the money, what would you do here?'

Rowan stared at him, 'You mean in this room?'

'We'll start here,' he answered calmly. 'Come on, cat got your tongue?'

Rowan gasped, then stammered, 'You need new lino and mats, you need new bright washable wallpaper. You need a new sink bench and cupboards—that thing is a disgrace, all the water whoops along the warps and pours on to the floor.' She was beginning to enjoy herself. 'You need a new vacuum cleaner and washing machine, and that fridge held together with curtain wire is pathetic.'

'Anything else?' He had a twinkle in his eye.

Rowan was mystified by his attitude. 'Yes, paint. Paint on the inside, paint on the outside, and carpets and curtains.'

'And who's going to do all this work if I get the material?'

'I will,' Rowan said rashly, not having the foggiest notion how to do it. 'And Jordan, and Drew would help me. They'd do anything to make life more pleasant for Regan.'

'Well, after you finish your meal you'd better start measuring up, hadn't you? I don't want any waste. We'll go to Nelson on Friday, if you're free, and we'll order everything you want. Now, finish eating your most excellent casserole.' He sat down and began to eat again.

Rowan sat down, but she was too overwhelmed to eat. 'You mean it, you really mean it?' she demanded in an awed voice.

'I rarely say anything I do not mean,' and Daniel McKinnon chuckled at her incredulous expression.

Stunned, Rowan tried to marshal her thoughts. He hadn't reacted at all as she had expected to her explosion. Perhaps her outrage had been because there had been a tiny bit of truth in his statement about her showing she was a better housekeeper than Regan. What a strange man!

'Why haven't you done anything about it before?' she demanded.

'I suppose I got into the habit of saving every penny and it's hard to change a lifetime of thrift. We had a hard time getting a footing here, then my wife and I decided to set every spare cent aside for Regan, so she might have a chance to use her God-given talents. I thought it would cost thousands of dollars and I wanted her to have the best. But she has won two different scholarships by her own efforts, so the money is there to be used.'

Rowan beamed at him. He was a darling in spite of his surly exterior. He had been doing it all for Regan. 'I'm so happy, I could dance a Highland fling if I had the music.'

Without a word he rose from the table and strode through to his bedroom. Minutes later Rowan heard the skirl of the bagpipes coming round the house and she ran out of the back door, just in time to see Daniel McKinnon take up his position on a corner of the cement square. Quickly pulling off her sneakers, Rowan ran to the centre stage. With a neat bow she picked up the beat and started to dance, delighted that her feet had not lost their cunning as she stepped and twirled, her eyes sparkling and face glowing.

As she completed the dance and bowed rather breathlessly to the piper, a loud clapping came from the gate and she discovered an audience of Jordan, Drew and a very excited Khan.

McKinnon tucked his pipes under his arm and said cryptically, 'Women should wear skirts, trousers are for the men.' He disappeared round the corner of the house.

'That was fantastic,' Drew was ahead of Jordan through the gate. 'You picked on the one thing to melt old Mac's heart. The pipes are his one indulgence, and he haunts the Highland Dancing Competitions.'

'It was such a fluke,' Rowan said laughing. 'I had no idea he played. I'll get my parents to send down my full costume. I used to dance in the Competitions myself years ago. It was fun.'

Jordan stood off, smiling. 'He may make disparaging remarks about your jeans, but I do not criticise perfection. How come you got so buddy-buddy? You were at daggers drawn at lunch time.'

'Oh, incredible things are happening. Can you help me measure up the kitchen for new cupboards, and how much paint do I need to paint the house, and will you both help me? I'm allowed a free hand.'

As she excitedly explained, both men volunteered their whole-hearted support and she saw their enthusiasm kindle at the thought of what a wonderful surprise it would be for Regan coming home. Her sister must be super-special to have these two prepared to give up all their free time to cheer her up.

Driving to Nelson on Friday with Daniel McKinnon sitting erect beside her in his dark Sunday-best suit, Regan felt that she would never in her lifetime make a more unusual trip. She had wanted to hate this man, she boiled with rage at the thought of his rejecting her as a baby, and here they were driving together, and there was no doubting his good will towards her. He was prepared to be generous, naming a limit far beyond her expectations, and by his wry comments she knew he intended to go around with her and take an active interest in the shopping spree.

'Why did you leave me and choose Regan when we were babies?' she was appalled to hear herself demand baldly.

She had meant to work up to it gradually, to soften him up, but it had just popped out.

'Have you felt hurt by that decision?' he asked gently, looking at her from under craggy eyebrows.

'Yes, I have,' she said thickly, trying to concentrate on her driving so that he wouldn't see her pain.

'I'm sorry. It was not intended to hurt you.' There was a prolonged silence before he spoke again. 'I was a twin, you know. My brother and I were identical twins. I was the younger, the last one born . . . the shadow twin. Did you know that there's always a stronger and more dominant twin, and a weaker one?'

Mutely, Rowan shook her head.

'Well, that is true. Tam was the leader and I the follower. Looking back, I don't believe I ever thought for myself, I was his shadow. I was not unhappy, mind you. Not until we grew up and separated. He, being the eldest, got the farm and I was sent to the city to earn my living. It was a bad time for me, like a bereavement—no, worse, as if I had died, but was still walking around, unable to function properly. At twenty I had to start growing up, beginning my development as if I was a child, and making terrible mistakes, until I began to see myself as a born loser.'

'But you weren't,' Rowan protested, trying to reassure him somehow.

'Not altogether, but I did not realise that until I came to this country and met Jenny and married her. Oh, I still made mistakes, but with her beside me they did not seem so bitter. You see, I was eaten with sourness. Tam at home with all the folks, the favourite, the merry one, the one with the farm and the brains, and how could he fail? And he had children, too. That was another failure— Jenny longed for children and we were not blessed with any.'

Rowan wanted to stop him from talking. His voice was

flat and unemotional, but she could hear the grief as if he was reliving the past.

'She nagged at me to adopt a child, for years she went on, but I was too proud. Then when I was forty I finally agreed, and almost immediately they called us and they offered us twins, identical twins. I couldn't face the prospect of rearing twins, so I asked for the youngest, the least strong one, to give it a chance to grow up free and whole.'

The tears were pouring down Rowan's face, and she slowed the car a little but kept driving. He hadn't rejected her, he had *chosen* Regan, that was entirely different.

'I have wonderful parents,' she said shakily.

'I'm pleased, very pleased. Don't cry, lass, I didn't mean to hurt you.' He patted her shoulder awkwardly as if he wasn't used to showing affection. 'I hoped you'd understand.'

'I do,' Rowan said in a husky voice. 'Did you ever think of me, and wonder if I'd turn up?'

'You were never far from my thoughts, and I prayed for you all these years, and I knew you would come. I've been waiting to see if I made the right decision. And I did, you know, and the guilt I've carried has rolled away. To see you walk in, so like Regan, yet sparky and confident with your cheerful smile and dancing ways. Yes, I was right. She was the shadow twin, but because you grew up separately she is a person in her own right. You're both fine girls; I hope you'll be friends.'

'We will be,' Rowan brushed away her tears and sniffed inelegantly, 'And I'm going to *enjoy* spending your money.'

He chuckled, 'I thought you might, but I'll be holding the cheque book. There'll be no extravagance.'

Rowan laughed and put her foot down harder on the accelerator. She felt a tremendous sense of freedom herself. If she had twins she wouldn't separate them, but she would be very careful to see that they both had an equal chance to develop their personalities. Imagine having twins the image of Drew . . . Away she went again, soaring on that wonderful upthrust of air. Oh, Drew, choose me, please choose me. Just because I'm stronger doesn't mean I don't need your love to lean on.

The day was a great success, and they packed enough in the car to be able to make an immediate start. Daniel McKinnon agreed that she could bring Aaron and Hannah with her if she wanted to work every day, and he treated her to a very fine lunch.

She rang her parents that night and they really rejoiced in her news of Regan, and of Mr McKinnon, and said that they intended to drive down for a visit, arriving on the first of the month. Rowan hung up thoughtfully. By then Drew would have settled his problems and maybe, just maybe, she would know if she was going to be part of his future. If he asked her to marry him, then her parents would be present to enjoy her happiness, and if it was Regan he chose, then they could help her to put the pieces together.

Khan followed her happily through to the lounge and flopped on the sofa beside her, his head resting on her knees. She sat glued to the TV until it went off. Even if a lot of it was rubbish, at least it stopped her thinking and trying to evaluate her chances of ending up as Mrs Drew Hewitt, or what would happen if Drew lost the Bonnie Doon in three weeks' time. The very worst thought was that he might wait till Regan came home, and then propose, and she would know forever she had been second choice again. How could she survive the next three weeks? Work, of course, so that she could sleep soundly at nights.

The first week simply rushed by and Rowan was amazed at what had been accomplished. On Sunday night she sat with Rochelle, watching Drew and Jordan cooking some steaks on the barbecue on her front lawn.

Rochelle smiled at her. 'I must have been born lazy,

nothing gives me greater pleasure than to watch someone else work, especially men. I thought Sunday was supposed to be a day of rest. Every bone in my body aches, but I've loved every minute. Thanks for including us in the trip.'

'Drew's idea, a reward for Aaron for helping on the farm this week. He's been such a great kid, no trouble at all. And look at Hannah, she's angelic when she's asleep, and dynamite when she's on her feet. The men are crazy about her, especially Mr McKinnon. I heard him laugh the other day, the first time ever, and went to look, and there was Hannah stealing back the toast I'd given her to feed the white rabbit. She's just so cute, and fast with it.'

'I'm going to write to Jim tonight,' Rochelle said quietly.

'What brought that on?' Rowan stared at her in surprise.

'Lots of things. The kids mainly. I've been watching Aaron with Jordan and Drew today. Look at him now, a man amongst men, only three yet he deliberately chooses their company. I feel I've deprived him of so much, I've been treating him like a baby. He needs his father's company, too. And I've robbed Jim of the pleasure of watching Hannah develop. He'd love her, too. And I miss him . . .'

'I'm glad,' Rowan replied wishing there was some action she could take to bring about her own happiness. But there wasn't, she just had to wait. Two weeks until the end of the month . . . Sometimes she wanted to move the clock forward so that she would know one way or the other, but mostly she just wanted time to stand still, like this morning in church, sitting between Drew and Daniel McKinnon, and this afternoon at the cave when they had become unexpectedly separated from the others and Drew had automatically reached for her . . .

'Dinner coming up,' Jordan announced. 'Hey, your phone's ringing, Rowan, don't talk too long.'

Rowan ran for the house. 'Hullo, Rowan here,' she gasped breathlessly.

'Regan McKinnon speaking. Hullo, sister, I love you, thanks for writing. I tried to write but there was so much to say . . .'

Rowan knew Regan was crying and she was too, pressing the phone so hard to her ear that it hurt. 'Where are you?'

'Australia,' she sobbed. 'This is crazy, I'm so happy, yet I can't think of anything to say.'

'Me neither.' Rowan was laughing and crying at the same time.

'I'm coming home.'

'When . . . how long . . . ?' Rowan demanded.

'For Dad's birthday on the first. In two weeks. Don't tell him, it's a surprise. There was an exhibition here and one of my paintings sold for a ridiculous price . . . so I'm coming home to meet you. I'll only stay two days, because I have the rest of the course to finish. We'll talk then, Rowan, we'll talk then. Give my love to Drew and Jordan. God bless you, Rowan. Goodbye.'

'Goodbye,' Rowan said, yet kept holding on as if there was more to come . . . but there wasn't. All those years apart, yet when they spoke they couldn't think of a thing to say.

She walked slowly back to the group, staring down at them, then she announced, 'That was Regan. She's coming home for her father's birthday. It's to be a surprise.'

'Why didn't you call me?' Jordan was on his feet. 'Did she give you a message for me?'

'She sent her love to you and to Drew.' Rowan sat down beside Drew and took her plate, but she couldn't eat. She hadn't had time to ask Regan which one she loved, but Regan had put Drew first. Who wouldn't?

'What else did she say? Come on, give,' Jordan glared at her.

'Nothing much. Oh, yes, she's sold a painting, I think for a big price, that's why she can fly home for two days. There was an exhibition . . . She'll have to go back to finish the course.'

'I knew she wouldn't be able to stay away from me too long,' Jordan said with supreme complacency. 'We'll have a party for old Mac, didn't you say your parents were coming down then, Rowan. We'll have to get the house finished. Wow! what a day. He must be a hundred. Time he retired, sitting on that block of land, doing nothing. I wouldn't mind a crack at it myself. What do you think, Drew? Now that the government is putting the new bridge in at Aorere, it should be money for jam.'

Rowan shivered and inched a little closer to Drew, loving just to be near him. Events were moving too fast for her. It was as if some mighty hand was drawing the strings of their lives together: hers and Regan's, her parents' and McKinnon's, Drew's and Jordan's and his mother's, and Rochelle's and Jim's—it was frightening, yet exciting. She didn't know if she wanted to fight the inevitability of it, to run and hide from it or to flow with it, as with the tide that moved up the bay.

Drew was discussing something with Jordan about farming, and then she heard him say, 'To quote Shakespeare, "There is a tide in the affairs of men, which, taken at the flood, leads on to fortune". Be ready for it, Jordan.'

Rowan threw Drew a startled glance, talk about being on the same thought track!

'I will be. And I'll be ready to meet Regan's plane when she lands from Aussie, too. I'll stay on after the meeting.'

'How did you know she was in Australia?' Drew demanded.

Jordan stood up laughing. 'Oh, you and McKinnon are

Babes in the Wood compared to me. Did you really think
you could keep Regan's whereabouts a secret from me?
I've known for a week. Here, Khan, you savage beast, get
your munchers into my steak and allow me to leave in
peace.' He scraped his meal off his plate to Khan who had
been watching the food disappear with anxious, but
well-behaved anticipation.

Rochelle sighed, 'That steak was fabulous, in fact the
whole day was. Thanks, Drew. Come on, Aaron, we must
go home, I've got a letter to write.'

Drew stood up. 'I'll carry Hannah for you. Won't be
long, Rowan, keep the fire warm.'

She threw another stick on the fire and watched the
sparks fly upward. That fire was easy to control, but the
one inside her burned brightly without any fuel being
added. It had happened so swiftly. She had met Drew,
fallen in love with him, and now could not imagine what
life would be without him in it. Love is a many-
splendoured thing . . . where had that thought come from?
No matter, that was just what her feelings were, that her
love for Drew was splendid and magnificent and awesome, greater than she had ever thought possible to
experience.

He would be back soon, he would sit with her by the
firelight, his arms would be around her and his lips would
find hers and she would experience happiness in that
moment that would be so intense that it would almost be
pain. She longed and yearned for him to say he loved her,
yet knew instinctively that Drew would not speak until he
felt the time was right, and she had to accept that unlike
hers, his mind might not be on a permanent, lasting
relationship, but just on the pleasure of the moment.

'Now that's what I call considerate, Rochelle and
Jordan taking themselves off like that and leaving us
alone. What a wonderful night, just look at the stars.'

Rowan gazed up at the star-spangled sky, and out

across the Bay mirrored silver in the moonlight, and then at the wild exotic flowers and fruits close by, before turning her eyes on Drew. 'If I could pull a switch and stop the world I'd do it now. It's so beautiful.'

'Not yet.' He reached for her and as his arms enfolded her, laughed. 'Not for years, I'm just starting to enjoy myself. If you like you can push the fast forward button to give these next two weeks a hurry-up.'

'Sorry, I'd forgotten you must be a bit tense about Bonnie Doon. But Regan's coming home, and that ought to counter-balance most of your difficult moments.'

'It's great news. We must get all the alternations done. Tell you what, I'll let the farm take care of itself and work with you each day. Regan won't be able to believe her eyes. Do you know, Jordan reckons you've mesmerised old McKinnon. How do you do it?'

'By looking like Regan. I'm just cashing in on the natural affection you all have for her. She must be a favourite with the whole district—I love the way people's faces crease into happy smiles when they see me. I only hope it lasts when she comes back; the genuine article as you once described her. What does that make me,' Rowan asked ruefully, 'just a carbon copy?'

'That must have been one of my more stupid remarks. I also told you, you are nothing like her—chalk and cheese, remember! You are an original, a delightful original.'

He kissed her and she was soaring again, higher and higher, until all the pain was left behind and only the ecstasy remained.

Someone must have pressed the fast forward button Rowan reflected on the last day of the month as she rushed around putting the finishing touches to the sparkling-clean house. Time seemed to have melted as each day she and Drew worked side by side, and Jordan joined them each evening. They had worked together, laughed together and achieved a miracle.

Drew and Jordan were now in Nelson at the meeting and Mr McKinnon hung about the house in a most disconcerting fashion. She wished he would find something to do as she wanted to complete the preparations for the surprise party.

'How about a cuppa?' she offered, even though lunch had not long been finished.

'Yes, that would be fine. I am worrying a little about Drew. This has always been his hardest day each year, and this time it will be even more difficult. I hope he wins through, he deserves that farm.'

'What about Jordan?'

'No. Jordan wants no part of it, he needs a greater challenge, something of his own.' He sighed deeply.

'You're missing Regan,' Rowan said with sudden perception.

'I suppose I am. She'll ring me tomorrow for my birthday, she won't forget. It will be very nice to have your parents for a visit, mind you.' He smiled as he accepted his tea. 'Although the way you've been filling those biscuit tins they must have hearty appetites. I'm thinking I'd rather keep them for a week than a fortnight.'

Rowan laughed. 'I'm just testing the new oven.'

'I was just teasing you. You've done a grand job here. I wish Regan could see it. But she'll he home soon enough, and to stay. It cheers me to think of having her live so close after she marries.'

Rowan felt the blood drain from her face, and hastily got up to check the oven . . . anything to cover up her dismay. Drew must have discussed his plans with Daniel McKinnon, . . . of course he would if he was planning to marry Regan. Oh, Drew, I've lost you, I've lost everything! I loved you so. It wasn't better to know the worst, it could kill you. And Daniel McKinnon was rambling on, he didn't even realise what he had said.

'Here, girl, you haven't had your tea. Stop fussing around, and sit down a while.'

Rowan sat down opposite the old man. He mustn't guess that she was slowly dying inside.

His gimlet-blue eyes fastened on her. 'What's the matter? You're pale as a ghost. You've been working too hard. No more today, that's an order.'

Gratefully Rowan fastened on the excuse. 'Yes, I'm a bit tired. Do you mind if I go home now? There's cold meat in the fridge for your tea.'

'Away with you this minute. You're always so busy thinking of others, never a thought for yourself. I cannot begin to thank you for all you've done, for me, for Drew and Jordan, and for Regan. Your parents will be thinking I'm a slave-driver. Go home and rest.'

Rowan held back the tears that threatened to overflow as she lifted the last lot of biscuits from the oven. 'Thanks. I'll be okay in the morning.' She would have to be, it was going to be a gala day with Regan and her parents there, and the birthday party. Thank God she had a short time to pull herself together.

Driving home to her house on the hill, she fought to keep her mind away from the thought of Regan and Drew . . . and failed. Only now was she beginning to realise that she had always believed it would work out right for her. The small warnings and odd negative thoughts had not touched the surface of her mind. It had always been a figment of her imagination, a fantasy, an exercise in futility. Oh, Drew . . .

Khan followed her into the bedroom, his ears pricked anxiously as he sensed her distress and as she flung herself across the bed and wept bitterly, he whined and whimpered in sympathy, but she was oblivious to his efforts.

Later, as she showered and changed into bright slacks and top, she glared at her pale face. Drew would call on his way home . . . to share his news with his good friend

Rowan, for that's all she was. Then she must be ready to congratulate him if he had won the Bonnie Doon or comfort him if he had lost. Her own loss would be well-hidden by careful application of make-up and a massive build up of pride.

Her parents were coming and with a little expert coaching would publish abroad their need for her to come home with them, and she would, with a great show of reluctance to leave her new-found friends, rush to pack her bags. Her chin lifted in determination. She had achieved what she had come for: she had made contact with Regan, she would soon meet her in the flesh, and she knew why Daniel McKinnon had left her, and understood. She had done more than that, she had found love, and lost it, and she wouldn't have missed the experience for the world, not even to avoid the pain and adjustment that she would have to go through in the next few months.

She walked out to the front porch and sat looking down on the calm, still water, gun-metal shot-silk today, because it was cloudy, but beautiful still. Her heart ached. She was not only losing Drew, but this house she had fallen in love with, and the view. Jordan had said 'Don't become a captive here in Golden Bay; it will never let you go'—but it had happened.

She looked out across the Bay to the sandstrip where the birds gathered, beyond to the huge stranded pine like a wrecked sailing ship, then farther across to the Dolomite works, like a sandstone stockade, four-square and golden against the blue bush-clad hills.

Around her sprawled the wonderful garden, grapefruit, lemon, wild passion-fruit; all the sub-tropical plants with their exotic flowers and ripe fruit; massed purple flowers of the lasiandra, orange chinese lanterns blooming where the bellbird sat, the nameless shrub with the Victorian posies, they all mingled with sweet roses and pansies.

As Khan began to bark she heard the station-wagon

take the hill and she prepared to meet Drew with a smile.
It wasn't his fault he couldn't love her. He came striding
round the corner of the verandah, pushing the excitedly
barking Khan to one side. He was smiling in a way that
almost shattered her carefully-held poise.

'Will you marry me, Rowan?' He caught her hands in
his and lifted her to her feet.

'What did you say?' she demanded in a trembling voice,
being positive she had not heard him correctly.

'I said, will you marry me, Rowan? Will you be my
wife? Will you spend your life on Bonnie Doon with me?'

She stared up at his handsome, confident smiling face,
and hope flared in her heart, and raced through her veins
like sparkling wine, then came a swift and sudden anger
blotting out everything else. 'No, Drew Hewitt, I won't
marry you. I want to be able to communicate with the
man I marry. How was I supposed to know you were
thinking of marriage? You've never said one word of love
to me.'

'You knew I loved you.' He was smiling down at her
outraged face, his eyes alive with laughter. 'Actions speak
louder than words . . .'

'Not in my book,' Rowan flung at him furiously. 'I'm no
Victorian Miss, to sit with hands folded in my lap waiting
on the sidelines for you to make all the decisions, and then
flutter my eyelashes and murmur, "This is so sudden!"'

He roared with laughter, and tried to pull her into his
arms. 'I've never seen you that way. I love you so much,
my darling Rowan, and I'm sorry I've upset you. I've had
no practice in proposing, and I've made a complete botch
of it. Forgive me. I just couldn't wait to get here, and I
collected a speeding ticket on the way. I haven't bought a
ring to put on your finger, and I should have chosen a
different setting, somewhere romantic . . . Let's start
again—we'll drive over to the Springs where I first discovered that I loved you . . .'

'It's not the ring, it's not the setting,' Rowan said stubbornly, fighting to hold on to her anger, knowing it was draining away, feeling again the upthrust of air current, the exhilaration, the exultation of her love for him.

'But you do love me?' he questioned, his voice soft, his grey eyes serious and intent.

'Yes, I love you, but it's not enough. If I marry you I want us to be able to talk. I admire the way you protect Regan and try to protect me, and sometimes I'll need your strength to lean on, but not all the time. I'm not fragile, I won't collapse if you let me share your problems. I want to be a true partner, for us to be open, to be able to say what we feel . . .'

'I'm saying what I feel, that I love you.' He was smiling again. 'And you are right about me keeping things to myself, but for many years it's had to be that way. It was the only way to survive in that household, not to show my feelings or my thoughts. If you're a little patient with me, I'll change.'

'Oh, Drew . . .' Her vivid blue eyes were brilliant with love and tenderness.

'Could we start practising now? I have this awful problem and I'm sure you could help me. You see, I was a crusty old bachelor and planning to stay that way and then suddenly I met this amazing girl, and I fell in love with her. She was so beautiful, so full of laughter and vitality, but a terrible flirt . . .'

'I was not!' Rowan said indignantly.

'You're supposed to be objective,' Drew informed her sternly. 'She flirted with my brother, and pretended she preferred his company, and drove me to distraction. I wanted to ask her to marry me, but my affairs were in such a mess, tangled up with other people's lives, and I couldn't speak until I'd straightened them out and had something to offer her. Then when I did ask her, she refused me. What should I do?'

'Oh, I wouldn't marry *her*, she sounds terribly selfish and totally lacking in understanding,' Rowan said with a breathless laugh.

'Ah, but I'm going to marry her,' Drew said, firmly pulling her into his embrace, and this time she didn't resist.

And she was soaring high above the earth, never to be a Gooney bird again. This was the love her father had spoken of; this rapture, this pure delight that binds with unbreakable cords the hearts of those who truly love each other.

Much later, Rowan asked, 'What about Regan? Will she be pleased about our engagement?'

'She'll think all her prayers have been answered. She would have loved you anyway, but when she sees the change in me, in Jordan, and in her father, her blue eyes will shine with that inner radiance and excitement and you'll find yourself believing in her miracles, too. Jordan will be with her now. I had a drink with him before he went to the airport, and even he was a bit awed at the way things have worked out, and it takes a lot to shake him. He said not to knock your halo off when I proposed.'

'But I've done nothing,' Rowan protested with a laugh.

'He thinks you have, and he's grateful, but he said you're not to presume on that. McKinnon has shed ten years since you arrived, so have I for that matter. I feel like a teenager in love.' And to prove it, he kissed her again.

Rowan's return to earth this time was aerodynamically perfect, the Gooney bird landings were over. 'But weren't you ever hurt that Regan preferred Jordan?'

'Not hurt, a little scared for her, maybe. He had such power to give her pain, but he won't do that now. He's really got his act together. He plans to go into partnership with McKinnon, to build a house through the gate from us, to develop that block across the river. He discussed it with McKinnon before the meeting.'

'And Mr McKinnon agreed!' Rowan gasped.

'Of course not, he's too cautious for that, but he said if Jordan felt the same way in six months, he'd discuss it then. On the strength of that Jordan voted with me so that he could get his capital free, and that's how I got free title to Bonnie Doon.'

'So that's what he meant about Regan living next door to him yesterday. I thought he meant she was going to marry you.'

Drew held her away from him. 'You're crazy. She's my mate, my kid sister, I told you that all along.' Then he smiled, and his grey eyes lit with wicked amusement. 'You're showing a shocking lack of faith in the man you're marrying. If I had wanted Regan, Jordan would have been no match for me.'

'Of course not, I just didn't think about it that way,' Rowan said, laughing with him.

'McKinnon will never forget this birthday party,' Drew remarked to Rowan the next afternoon. 'Neither will the rest of the district. It's everybody's party—our engagement, Daniel's birthday, and Regan returning a celebrity.'

Rowan surveyed the incredible scene, the happy, laughing people overflowing the house and the neatly mown lawns, cards filling every available space at the McKinnons' and the Hewitts', and the boundary gate wide open to welcome them in.

'I can't believe it. It's as if the whole world is celebrating. A golden day in Golden Bay. When the news of Regan winning that top painting award in Australia hit the headlines this morning she rang him immediately. She wanted to surprise him with it, but the radio and newspapers beat her to it. Then the phone never stopped ringing, and McKinnon invited each one who rang to his now unsurprise party this afternoon to congratulate her personally. My mother and father are loving it all, but I've hardly had time to talk to Regan . . .'

'Do you mind?' Drew asked.

'Not at all, I've got you.' Rowan's vivid blue eyes were brilliant with happiness. 'It was fantastic meeting her, we loved each other on sight, just like I had imagined we would.'

Drew smiled at her. 'I find it incredible that she bought her dress and shoes in Sydney, and you got yours in Auckland, and you meet here in identical kit. Jordan felt he had to put name tags on you to assist the visitors, or so he said. I knew he got mad when people began congratulating Regan on her engagement to me.'

'You have no trouble telling us apart?' Rowan demanded anxiously.

'None at all. I'll nip out and get your gear from your father's car. McKinnon is telling everyone you're going to dance the Highland fling for his birthday, and they're waiting to see it.'

Rowan watched him stride for the gate and moved to join her parents, Jordan and Regan and McKinnon. 'Drew says to warm up your pipes,' she warned the birthday man.

Jordan put an arm around each girl. 'People keep asking me how I can tell you two apart. I just answer that it's not my problem. I grab the first one who comes by and kiss her, and if she smacks my face, it's Rowan.'

'You're an idiot,' Rowan declared.

'I'm not. I can tell you apart, but can Drew?' His eyes sparkled with malicious amusement. 'Let's run a test on him. Quickly, before he gets back.'

Jordan took the name tags and exchanged them. 'Now, Regan, you stand with Rowan's parents, and I'll drape my arm possessively over you, Rowan, and we'll see who he hands the case to.'

Rowan wanted to protest. It was an unfair test, Drew

wasn't expecting it, and with Jordan's arm about her . . .

'It's okay, Rowan, Drew doesn't make mistakes,' Regan said quietly, as Drew came towards them smiling.

Rowan held her breath. Dear God, let him choose me or I'll feel like a Gooney bird for the rest of my life.

Drew put the case down and looked around the silent group, then grinned. 'Take your hands off my girl, Jordan, she has to dance.'

Rowan felt herself soaring upward. Drew was right, Jordan would never be a match for him, and with shining eyes she moved to take her case.